Due

Mr. Teach Goes to War

MR. TEACH
GOES TO WAR

by Frank A. Cooper

Whittlesey House
McGraw-Hill Book Company, Inc.
NEW YORK   TORONTO   LONDON

Library of Congress Catalog Card Number: 57-6388

Published by Whittlesey House
A division of the McGraw-Hill Book Company, Inc.
Printed in the United States of America

To Ruth

1

IT LACKED about an hour of noon when young schoolmaster Hosea Bonesteel—he was just turning nineteen—told himself that what he needed most was a big breath of fresh air. He clattered down from behind his tall desk, flicked his restless eyes once over his class of pioneers' sons, and strode to the open window. Striking his large palms on the sill, he thrust his thick body far out and pulled into his lungs the moist odors of early spring. His eyes brightened.

Bonesteel breathed again. Into his nostrils came the fresh sweet smell of the waters of the great Lake Champlain a half mile away, that smell that was new again because the ice had so recently gone out. He smiled and listened. In the half-distance he heard the flooded Saranac River rumbling into the lake.

"Good," Bonesteel said to himself. "All good!"

He lifted his nose to the cleared land nearby, to the blackened stump-lot beyond, and finally to the dark green wall of the forest.

A light breeze brought to him the odors of pines, hemlocks, and cedars. He filled his chest again. . . . Ah,

7

the forest. Hundreds of miles of it to the north, south, west—with the lake to the east. New land. Free people, good people, good men. This was the place for a good school and a good teacher in that school, a place where boys could be taught to become good men.

Suddenly Bonesteel's eyes darkened. His thoughts turned to the war with England that had been going on for two years now—the War of 1812—the Second War of Independence, some people called it.

Everybody said that the British would soon come from the north through that forest, up that lake and on to Plattsburg. What would the war do to all this that he loved so much? Did he have to ask? He growled deep in his throat like a faithful watchdog.

A few of the boys looked up. Bonesteel turned his eyes particularly toward two of them: Joshua Benson and that half French-Canadian, half Indian boy everybody was calling Muskrat Jack. Jack and Joshua were grinning at each other.

That set Bonesteel to thinking about Jack. A few months ago Jack's drunken French-Canadian father had brought this half wild sixteen-year-old son of his to school, made arrangements with Bonesteel to look after his son, and had then slunk away. Jack had not seen his father since.

And then Bonesteel thought of the time when he was buying some horn buttons in Joshua's father's store. Joshua was waiting on him. Naturally they got to talking about Jack.

Bonesteel was saying, "I want to get Jack so he'll talk to me, Joshua, talk to me freely."

8

Joshua said, "He sure don't talk much to anybody except me."

"That's a fact. All he says to me is 'Yes, Teach,' 'No, Teach.' And mighty sullen even then."

"Yep." Joshua's eyes were very serious and very kind.

"I can't do anything for him when he acts like that. Can I?"

"Well, no sir. You certain can't."

"Well, don't you think—"

But sympathetic Joshua did not let him finish. "You're different from any man Jack has ever known. And this is a different place from the way he's used to living."

"Different?"

"With his father on the *Black Sloop*. And with the Carcajou."

Bonesteel growled, "The Carcajou!" Then he sighed, "Jack misses his father. Doesn't he?"

Joshua smiled that honest smile that Bonesteel liked so much to see. "You sure don't know how much, Mr. Bonesteel. But just give him time to get used to you. Then you'll see."

Bonesteel remembered that he had almost shouted the word "Time!" and that then he had calmed down some and had wondered why Joshua had grinned when he said, "I'm a patient man, Joshua. I can wait—I can wait."

" 'Wait' it is, Mr. Bonesteel."

"Oh, I notice Jack doesn't carry his knife any more. I've heard he's an expert with it."

"At throwing. Yes sir. He carries it in his shirt now. Not outside. But that's a good sign."

9

Bonesteel looked at Joshua a long time. At last he said, "I believe you're right, Joshua. I believe you're right."

"I know I am."

"All right. I'll go on that."

And Bonesteel remembered how much comfort that conversation with Joshua had given him.

Schoolmaster Bonesteel jolted himself back from his memories into the present. He turned back to his desk. He eyed his hourglass sourly and snapped it impatiently with his thick finger to hurry downward the last grains of sand. Then, satisfied that he had hastened time, he turned and thumped mightily upon his desk.

"Time's up, young gentlemen. Examination's done. Summer's come. Bring your labors up here to me. Step lively."

When all the boys had returned to their seats to hear what Mr. Bonesteel would say to them before dismissing them for the summer, they saw him take his time, fold his heavy arms over his barrel chest, and tip back his shaggy head. He didn't know that all this made him look more rugged to them, and that they liked him all the more for it. Nor did he know that they liked him all the more for the twinkle he was now trying to keep out of his eyes because he was working up to something good that they already knew all about.

Bonesteel made a great racket in his throat. He said, "Now, young gentlemen, I have something of an exciting nature to discuss with you." He put on a great scowl, and puffed away an early spring fly buzzing around his nose. "Well now—this certain something of an exciting nature—is—ahem—the 'wrassle,' as you call it, that I promised you when you came in here last fall with your heads as empty as a dry well, and when one after another of you tried to lick me. Remember?"

The boys' eyes lit up.

"Oh ho! I see you do remember. And I presume you remember also that I promised this 'wrassle' would be held on the very day this school would close for the summer. Which is today! Today, between any two of you and myself!" This last he shouted with a joyful whoop.

Now the boys were talking excitedly among themselves. Bonesteel had to shout. "The reward to your two gladiators is a cruise with me in my catboat, the *South Wind*." He laughed, "The British can wait for this one. Come, come. Waste no more time. Put up your men."

Bonesteel was happy. A boy was standing up and trying to be heard. The talk was dying down. "Mr. Bonesteel, we didn't forget. We got Joshua Benson and Muskrat Jack. We thank you, sir."

Bonesteel seized the desk. Muskrat Jack! No doubt the only fights he had ever seen were between vicious men—grudge fights. Probably never been in a sporting fight himself. How would he take this one? Can't let him win. He's an Indian. What little respect he might have would turn to contempt. Can't beat him either. He's an Indian, again, and it would be hate. Bonesteel's

11

knuckles turned white as he realized that either way he would lose.

But already the class was making for the door. Then only Jack and Joshua remained.

Jack was coming toward Bonesteel. Bonesteel blinked hopelessly. Jack was reaching into his shirt, drawing out his knife, and was laying the knife upon Bonesteel's desk. What did this mean? Joshua shrugged his shoulders, but he really looked worried.

Distantly, through the open window, Bonesteel could hear the waiting boys yelling and scuffling. In here everything was quiet.

Now Jack was speaking stiffly. "We fight our best, Teach. But all cannot win. Is it not?" He stood there for a moment haughtily looking off into space. Then he turned and, with the natural lithe motion of a young deer, bounded from the room.

Bonesteel shoved his hands into his pockets, looked down at the knife, then up at Joshua now grinning broadly at him from the doorway.

Bonesteel's lips formed the words, "Maybe, just maybe, it's going to work out all right."

Joshua, still grinning, nodded vigorously.

Even before Bonesteel stepped outdoors a few loitering soldiers and militiamen from the forts across the river had collected to see what was going on. Among them were Brigadier General Macomb and the tall Matthew Standish, a local blacksmith and preacher who sometimes made dangerous trips north to Canada to find out what the British were going to do next.

If Bonesteel had had his wits about him he might have wondered about these two men standing and talking there together. And he might have wondered, also, about a tall scornful hook-nosed stranger standing aloof watching Macomb and Standish. But he didn't.

Instead, he shouted, "Let's go!" and plunged in among the boys.

Jack threw himself against Bonesteel's knees. Bonesteel leaped aside and seized Joshua around the waist. Jack leaped again, and connected. All three went down in a whirling mass of arms and legs.

The fight was very fast. First one, then another, tore himself loose, only to leap back into it again. Now the boys had Bonesteel down. But with chest heaving and eyes wide he managed to gasp, "No you don't!" throw them off, and leap to his feet. But he was down again, and he began to wonder if he hadn't got hold of two bear cubs. But at least Jack was fighting fair and had not yet lost his temper.

Then it was that Bonesteel heard someone mutter, "Filthy barbarians!" He looked up and for an instant his eyes locked with those of the hook-nosed stranger, and he knew the man was talking about him and the boys. Then he heard Standish say, "Did I hear you aright, stranger?"

But Bonesteel was too busy to see the stranger toss his head arrogantly, or to see his long thin nose quiver with

13

hostility. And Bonesteel missed Standish's soft-voiced
" 'Filthy barbarians,' eh? Don't believe I got your
name?"

But now Bonesteel snapped a scissors hold on Jack and
was able to pant, "Stay right there, stranger. I'll be
through here presently."

The stranger started to move away. Standish's voice
stopped him. "What's your hurry, stranger? Bonesteel
here claims he has an appointment with ye."

Several men now turned to look. The stranger's natural pink complexion faded. His hot blue eyes took them
all in. Bonesteel saw this and in the back of his mind
formed the quick opinion that here was a very dangerous
man. And in that same instant Bonesteel was able to
pin Joshua's arms. With a scissors on Jack and holding
Joshua tightly he was momentarily the victor.

He did not wait to see how long he could hold the
boys. He leaped up. "Now," he panted, "if the stranger
will oblige me? We're not exactly filthy barbarians
around here."

He watched the stranger jerk off his fine broadcloth
coat and angrily roll up his sleeves. He heard him spit
out the words, "I don't know how I got into this, schoolmaster, but now that I am in, it won't last long."

"You got into this because you talk too much."

The two men started circling each other: Bonesteel
carefully, the stranger eagerly, animal-like, with a confident sneer on his face. Instinct told Bonesteel that
he had a fight on his hands this time. He sensed that the
crowd knew it too.

Suddenly Bonesteel felt powerful arms around his waist, felt himself lifted clear, and slammed hard upon the ground. Hazily he saw the stranger's feet coming at his face. He had just enough strength to roll away. The stranger tried again. Bonesteel gritted his teeth, lifted his feet, caught the man in the stomach, and heaved him away. But it must have been that the stranger knew how to fall, because Bonesteel heard Macomb say to Standish, "The stranger is able."

"But Hosea is real tough, General. Real tough." That was Standish's loyal reply. It made Bonesteel feel better.

So Bonesteel must now struggle to his feet. Encouraging hands were patting him on the back. The stranger was getting up too, and seemed more cautious.

The stranger started shuffling in, though, dangerous and menacing, and again Bonesteel knew he could not be quick enough. A vicious blow stung him on the mouth, and another crashed into his stomach. He hadn't even seen them coming. He knew he was badly hurt. He couldn't keep his knees from sagging. But they were all watching him: Matthew Standish, the General, Joshua and Jack—ah yes, Jack. For Jack he must not go down. Half blinded with pain, fighting for the breath that would not come, he must lash out. He felt his fist connect squarely with the stranger's jaw. He had the satisfaction of seeing the stranger's distorted face fade backward in a grimace of surprise and pain. He heard the crowd breathe, "Ah!" And Jack's voice surely must be among them.

But suddenly everything changed. Before Bonesteel could follow up, somebody out of nowhere rode his lathered horse between him and the stranger, threw himself off in front of the General, and shouted, "Glad I found ye, General, by gravy I am. Report from Cumberland Head—sir."

When Bonesteel got through blinking he saw the General was smiling. "You're doing fine. Let's have it."

"Yes sir! Anyway, there's a British fleet just passed Cumberland Head."

The General's smile vanished. "Go on."

"Wind's light. Couldn't tell where they's bound."

The General nodded.

"Likes as not they's figuring on Plattsburg. Or likes as not they's figuring to slog on south. Watched 'em from the road as I come here. Couldn't seem to make up their slimy minds."

Bonesteel heard the General say, "What have they got?"

"I don't know. Five sloops and thirteen galleys, I guess."

Bonesteel was listening carefully now. Although the General was talking to the crowd he seemed to be talking most to him. Was it because he hadn't wanted to believe all the talk about the British? About the possibility of an invasion?

The General was speaking rapidly. "The Redcoats didn't waste any time getting on the lake after the ice went out. This may be a raid like last year, or it may be a lot more. That's quite a fleet they've got."

Bonesteel felt the crowd tighten up like men pulling

in their belts before they're going to fight somebody. He looked at Jack. Jack was scowling at the stranger, who was studying the General.

The General continued. "You men return to the forts across the river. They've probably seen the fleet." He turned to the man who had brought the news. "Mister, give me your horse. You'll find her at headquarters at Cumberland Head, or somewhere along the way if I wind her. If she's yours you'll be paid. You militiamen own your own equipment, as a rule. You've done well. What's your name?"

The man gave his name. Then he said, "Me and my ma has got us a farm——" The General cut him off. Bonesteel laughed nervously with the crowd.

"All right. I'll remember." There was a hard grin on the General's face as he vaulted into the saddle. "I'm getting to Burlington somehow. Captain Macdonough's fleet is up Otter Creek at Vergennes with not a mast up yet. Sitting duck for those Redcoats."

Bonesteel heard someone shout, "Maybe that's what they're after."

A voice far back in the crowd cut in like a knife. "That's ridiculous."

The General leaned far out in his saddle. He was speaking directly at the stranger. "Is it? How do you know?"

It satisfied Bonesteel to see the stranger squirm. "Well, I——"

"All right," the General snapped. "You don't. But, for the information of all, I've got cannon at Burlington which I can move mighty quick. I'll give those Redcoats a stomachful if they get sassy. . . . Standish, you arouse the town. Ring the bell." He turned and grinned down at Bonesteel. "Schoolmaster, if I had a boy I'd send him to you. In the meantime, save some of that grit for a better cause. We're going to need you."

Then the General was gone.

A moment later the Academy bell was voicing the raucous clamor of "War—war!"

It had all happened so quickly. There was the fight, and then this excitement about the war. Now there were Joshua and Jack again. But Jack was looking past Bonesteel, a sneer upon his face.

Bonesteel was dismayed. Then he felt someone tap him roughly upon the shoulder. He turned. It was the stranger, putting on his coat but taking time to spit out the words, "We'll meet again, schoolmaster. And I hope those boys will be with you, especially that young savage there."

Turning quickly, the stranger lost himself in the crowd.

When Bonesteel looked back at Jack he saw the light of battle in his eyes. "Let him go, Jack," he said quietly. "I dare say we will meet him again."

Jack's mouth was pulled down in an ugly expression. "That man bad. But you real man. By ding you fight, Mister Teach."

"*Mister* Teach?"

Jack grinned broadly. "I call you *Mister* Teach now. I like you."

2

THE NOTE was carefully addressed and carefully folded. Bonesteel knew the sender even before he looked at the handwriting. It was Mr. Wall, who was the principal and only other teacher of the Academy. "Do come over this evening, Hosea," the note said. "I will be running bullets for the invasion." Bonesteel grinned as he looked forward to seeing his friend, the gentle Mr. Wall, doing such a warlike thing. But when he appeared at Mr. Wall's door he could not quite understand the greeting he got.

"Oh, so it *is* you, Hosea."

Bonesteel was puzzled. "Yes, it's me all right." He felt gingerly of his puffed lips and swollen eye.

Mr. Wall looked furtively up and down the street. "Er—yes, yes. . . . Now, quickly, come into the kitchen with me. I presume you don't want to be seen." Mr. Wall lowered his candle, and plucked nervously at Bonesteel's sleeve. Bonesteel followed, wondering about the reproving expression on Mr. Wall's face.

By the time they reached the kitchen Bonesteel was frowning. "Did you see the fight I got into?"

Mr. Wall's look of reproof deepened. "Er—no."

"You didn't? You didn't get a look at that stranger?"

Mr. Wall put the candle on the table, and pointed to one of the two chairs by the great fireplace. "Sit down, Hosea. I came home as soon as I saw what was going on."

Mr. Wall sat down in the other chair and reached into the fireplace for the ladle of melted lead. He poured a thin stream into the bullet mold.

Bonesteel watched the candlelight play on the silvery stream and on the polished brass mold. "You left?" he said.

Mr. Wall took his time to work the ladle back into the coals. Then, while holding the mold to let the bullet harden, he sat back to look soberly at his guest. Hosea frowned again. Mr. Wall leaned forward, opened the mold, and rolled the glistening bullet out upon the hearth. "Hosea, this may be the wrong time to speak about that Indian boy, Muskrat Jack. But your tussle with him this morning, and that other fight it led to, compels us to do so."

"I guess I don't quite follow you after all."

"You are a very young man, Hosea, and somewhat—impetuous?"

"I wasn't aware of it."

"So for the moment we will overlook the—the—"

"Lack of dignity of the whole business?"

Mr. Wall sighed and reached for the ladle again. "It was *entirely* undignified."

Bonesteel raised his eyebrows.

Mr. Wall continued. "There are some people in

Plattsburg who would disapprove to the extent of associating you with Muskrat Jack—as his *personal* friend, we mean."

Bonesteel jerked a nod. "I see, sir. And what would they say if they knew that is just what I want?"

"Hosea, as a teacher, you cannot afford to befriend every frontier waif who comes along. You must concentrate your efforts only upon the sons of our *worthy* citizens."

"Well, sir, I simply don't agree with you."

"We are building a new community up here in the North Country, a new community of the right kind of people. There are some great names here already."

"No argument there. But—"

Mr. Wall's delicate nostrils dilated. "And that Muskrat Jack has no place in it. Nor do we want his like."

Bonesteel decided it was time to control himself. With an effort he turned to persuasion. "I believe Jack has the qualities which a new community very much needs. Don't you think it's our job to bring them out?"

"Jack's blood and background are totally undesirable! His father, the Pilot, is a worthless beast, cast off even by the frontier."

"Well, if Jack hasn't got a good father, he's got to have somebody, I'm a-thinking."

Mr. Wall held up his hand. "And this half-breed son of his is the product of that decayed man and a St. Francis Indian squaw." Bonesteel saw the small red anger spots appear high upon Mr. Wall's cheekbones. "The Indian is a degenerate race. And the degeneracy of the Indian is in that boy!"

21

"Oh now, I don't agree with you there at all!" Bone-steel was getting a little angry again.

Mr. Wall was snapping his fingers impatiently now. "Oh, but you must!"

"Perhaps it is the Carcajou's hold on Jack's father that you fear more than you do Jack's Indian blood. Are you afraid the Carcajou will influence Jack through Jack's father?"

"The Carcajou? The bloody scoundrel! Yes, we'll add that to Jack's other disqualifications. We know that Jack's Indian blood will be only too receptive of the Carcajou's wickedness."

"Ridiculous!" Bonesteel laughed harshly.

"Laugh if you wish, Hosea! But it will be the Carcajou, and that other one: Laroque, the former Paris physician turned cutthroat."

"That's what the French Revolution did to a lot of them."

"Faugh! Those men have scoured this lake for several years now. And everywhere they go there are lawlessness and violence."

"There's no doubt they are a bad lot, but—"

"We have prayed that it be not so. But this is a raw, undeveloped country, and God in His infinite wisdom allows these evil men to remain yet a while to try us. But that does not mean that we should increase their wicked power by giving the white man's education to a half-breed who will one day join them."

"I don't like them any more than you do. But that doesn't—"

22

"Well then," Mr. Wall interrupted triumphantly, "you must see my point when I remind you that Jack's drunken father is the pilot for these cutthroats on their filthy boat—the *Black Sloop*, I believe they call it."

"But the Pilot is weak! Jack is strong!"

"On the contrary, the son will follow the father. He may do it openly, or he may do it treacherously—which would be even worse for you."

Bonesteel remembered Joshua's warning that Jack thought like an Indian. But he said, "I'm not afraid of that."

"I am. There is a strong attachment between them. And Muskrat Jack *is* Indian. Don't forget that, Hosea."

"Part Indian," Bonesteel said truculently.

Mr. Wall snorted. "One drop of Indian blood—total treachery."

Bonesteel opened his eyes wide and asked innocently, "Aren't you being a bit inconsistent, sir?"

"How am I?"

"When the Pilot brought Jack to us at the Academy you agreed to let Jack stay. You thought it was a good idea then."

"That was in a moment of sentimental weakness."

"I'd call it a moment of Christian strength, sir."

"You—er—thank you, Hosea. Thank you. But I have since reminded myself that life is not made up of sentiments. I simply made a mistake."

"I don't think so."

"Now I know Jack will run true to form."

"I'm sorry you believe that."

"Nor can you let your name become associated in any way with these ruffians, even secondhand through Jack. . . . Oh yes, we have decided to put it strongly to Joshua Benson's father also. He is a careful man."

Bonesteel leaped up. "Don't do that, Mr. Wall, I beg you!"

Mr. Wall closed his eyes and shook his head vigorously. "All the more reason."

"Why, man alive! Joshua may be the only lasting hold we have on Jack."

"I'm sorry. We speak from considerable public opinion."

Bonesteel's patience was at an end. "Well, suppose you do. You've got to be willing to stand up and be counted for what you believe is right, once in a while."

Mr. Wall got up wearily and put his hand on Bonesteel's shoulder. "These are troublous time for me, my boy. . . . This war. . . . Don't make it more difficult."

Bonesteel was too angry to see that Mr. Wall had really tried. He shrugged the hand away. "Sir, I intend to do all I can for Jack. He's worth saving. I have made up my mind."

It was then that Bonesteel saw Mr. Wall stiffen. "Then sir, it is fortunate that the school is dismissed for the summer. You will have time to think this matter over calmly without having to confuse your mind with any further ruffian displays on the school premises. But if, in the fall, you have not discovered that we are right—perhaps another position—"

24

3

THE BRITISH dawdled around Cumberland Head for a while, then sailed on south. They burned a farm on the Bouquet River, killed a man out fishing on the lake, sailed across the lake and fired on Fort Cassin guarding the mouth of Otter Creek. But the alert General had already reinforced the fort with his cannon from Burlington. The British got the stomachful the General had promised. They sailed back to the northern end of the lake—or so everybody thought —and Macdonough's fleet was saved.

That was the war in the North Country: raids and retreats on both sides. A few muskets fired, a few cannon balls hurled, a little property sent up in smoke, a few people killed.

Nothing accomplished, except fear. But fear was growing, and naturally Bonesteel was nervous about it.

That was why Bonesteel had said to himself that he wanted to make the cruise Jack and Joshua had won the kind of adventure they would always remember.

So now, by the light of a small fire and the quarter

moon overhead, they were loading the *South Wind*.

"Mister Teach."

Bonesteel looked up from the cockpit. "What is it, Jack?"

"The fusee, you take it, no?" Jack smiled and held out Bonesteel's gun.

Bonesteel smiled back. "You be responsible for it, Jack. It couldn't be in better hands."

But Jack seemed to know how much Bonesteel valued his gun. "It is beautiful fusee. But no, better you take it."

"You've got sharp eyes in your head and I'm thinking a soft heart in your breast, haven't you, boy?"

Good-natured Joshua was enjoying it all.

Jack said, *"You* take it. For me, the knife."

Bonesteel would take nothing seriously. "My father won the Battle of Saratoga with that gun. But if it will make you feel any better, I'll take it." He held out his hand.

The conversation dropped off and they continued loading in silence, each one contented in his own way. But then Joshua spoke before he thought. "Mr. Bonesteel, do you think there's a chance we'll run into the Carcajou at Valcour Island?"

Bonesteel saw Jack stiffen, and saw that, too late, Joshua realized what he had done. Bonesteel tried to cover it up. He snapped his gun to his shoulder and sighted it. "I doubt it, Joshua. Nobody knows exactly where the Carcajou is right now. But anyway, our cruise doesn't include Smuggler Bay, where he sometimes hangs out.

We are going to stay on this side of the island." He lowered his gun and made an exaggerated wink at Jack. "Though I must confess, I would like nothing better than to fill that blasted Carcajou with a goodly charge of rock salt and pig bristles."

"Better buckshot," Jack said bitterly.

"Buckshot, eh?" Bonesteel tried to keep his voice light.

Jack fingered his knife. "He bad to my father. But I do not fear him."

Bonesteel said, "Hand me that beanpot, Jack. I'm looking forward to some of those beans."

"So am I," Joshua said, trying to help get things back to normal.

"Call your dog, Jack," Bonesteel said. "He's part of this expedition too."

They hurried the rest of the duffle aboard. But just as Jack's dog, Little Loup, was settling himself confidently in the cockpit, Jack came to Bonesteel at the tiller.

"I do not wish to spoil cruise. I talk too much."

"About the Carcajou and your father?"

"Yes."

"Tell me, Jack, do you want to leave us and go back to your father?"

Jack's lips barely formed the words. "Yes, Mister Teach, very much."

"Then why don't you? There's probably no better time than now."

"For one, I don't know where *Black Sloop* is. The

Carcajou is in very bad business and don't tell."

"Go on, Jack."

"For two, my father told me I must stay with you."

Bonesteel was surprised. "Told you you *must?*"

"Yes. But I know you do not like my father, no?"

"Well, I—"

"So I tell you, I love my father very much, the way he live I hate. The Carcajou make him live that way. I have try to get my father away from the Carcajou. I have fail." Jack touched the knife under his shirt. "Someday I think I kill the Carcajou. You brave man. You understand."

Bonesteel could only expel his breath and say, "I see." Then he called out, "Cast off, Joshua."

The *South Wind* drifted down the inlet. The night wind caught, the boat heeled, the black waters of Cumberland Bay slipped smoothly out from under her transom, and they all sat silent under the old spell of a drawing sail curving up into the darkness. Gratefully, Bonesteel let it be that way for a while. At last he spoke. "Jack, why do your people call him the Carcajou?"

Jack's eyes shifted in the moonlight. "If you wish, Mister Teach. Though I do not myself choose to speak of these things."

"It's not good to keep things like that in your heart alone."

"Indian keeps many things in his heart alone," Jack said briefly.

Bonesteel was dismayed. The boat sailed on. Then Jack spoke suddenly. "You do not laugh, so I will tell.

Indian people very old. They know many things."

"Oh yes, indeed. Many things."

"The Carcajou is the wolverine. Not many wolverines in these forests now. My grandfather say they have gone to the Far North, to the great white snow."

"That's right. Not many around here now." Bonesteel was feeling better.

"The wolverine, she is the most strong of all the animal. One of these wolverine, a little longer but not so high as Little Loup, is strong as the bear. You believe that, Mister Teach?"

"Yes. I believe that."

"Not even two bears so foolish as to attack this one small animal."

Bonesteel nodded. "That's right. I've seen that myself."

Jack leaned forward. "And the wolverine has what you call very bad disposition. What he cannot carry off or destroy he make foul for no use any more."

"I've seen that too."

"And he is so wise and evil that he can destroy good Indian trap line, and drive good Indian away. My people know this."

Bonesteel nodded again.

Jack's voice dropped. "My people say the wolverine is the animal the Evil One put the ghost of the dead trapper into, like the dead trapper who hate other men. So when the wolverine comes he is sign of death. So my people call this evil man the Carcajou."

"So your people think this Carcajou is supernatural?"

29

"Yes sir, Mister Teach. Does he not escape all tries to catch him?"

"Well—nobody's caught him yet. That's true."

"Does he not make foul anything he cannot carry off?"

"I suppose he does."

Bonesteel saw that Jack was breathing hard, and that the whites of his eyes were showing.

Joshua was stirring uneasily. "Gosh, Jack. Do you really think that he is a carcajou like the wolverine? A ghost?"

Jack scrubbed his hand over his face. "Sometime I think it is not safe to say I don't believe. Sometime—"

Bonesteel had had enough. "I guess it's about time I put my oar in."

Both boys looked at him as though he had come from another world. "Sometimes in the night like this, when you feel so helpless on the lake, a superstition looks like the real thing. But it shouldn't. There are so many good influences around us."

There was fear in Jack's voice. "Oh, but Mister Teach!"

Bonesteel laughed reassuringly. "In an hour the sun will come up. Then tell me what you think. No offense to your people, Jack."

Bonesteel looked up at the sail, and beyond to the lightening sky. There was so much good in the world. Jack must have his share of it. He laughed as he thrust his hand into his shirt. He drew out two leather pouches which he laid on the seat beside him. Hooking his arm over the tiller, he took up his gun. This he charged with powder from his powder horn. Then he asked,

"Jack, what is in these two pouches?" There was a twinkle in his eye as he watched Jack pick up the heavier one and feel it.

"But of course, this one is buckshot."

"And the other?"

Jack pinched it and shook his head. "I do not know."

"Look in it."

Jack looked and gasped. "Rock salt and pig bristles! Oh, but Mister Teach, this would only make him mad."

"Undoubtedly. But I'll wager he wouldn't sit down for some time. I've used it on varmints before. It's very convincing."

Bonesteel poured a portion of the odd mixture into a piece of wax paper, twisted the paper up, and rammed the twist into his gun. He laughed heartily at the expressions on both boys' faces. "Now don't expect anything to come of this crazy idea, but it's good medicine for your fears."

Jack slapped his hand over his mouth. "Oh yes, it is very funny, if he don't never hear about it."

"He won't. Don't worry. I just did it to loosen us up. I guess it did. You're both laughing now."

Bonesteel laid the gun aside and looked toward the east. "Look. The sun is coming up. If you really want to know how much good there is in the world, all you have to do is watch a Lake Champlain sunrise." He paused, then said, "Come on, Joshua, take it from there."

Joshua looked around. "All right. . . . Seems as though the wind has dropped."

"Good. It often does that at sunrise, especially when

it's going to be beautiful. . . . Watch the deep violets turn to reds. There! It's beginning."

Jack asked Bonesteel, "It say something to you, Mister Teach?"

"It says something to me, Jack, I'm not ashamed to say."

Joshua said, "The sky is beginning to look like it's on fire."

Jack looked at Bonesteel again. "Many times my father and me watch the sunrise together."

Surprised, Bonesteel nodded. "Did it say something to him, Jack?"

"Yes. He say so."

"That's good. That's very good. . . . Look there. The reds are turning to orange now."

"He say, if the sunrise last all day he wouldn't have no more troubles any more."

"I like that."

Jack smiled.

Joshua said, "Now the orange is turning to yellow—like new leather."

Bonesteel was pleased. "Why, that's right. Like good new leather. Anything more, Joshua?"

"Yes. Those long clouds over Mt. Mansfield have got edges of silvery gold."

Bonesteel felt real contentment. "You're getting quite poetical, Joshua."

Jack said, "My father say to me, 'Never forget when we watch the sunrise together, Jack boy.' That's what he say."

Bonesteel spoke gently. "I'm beginning to think I had the wrong idea about him. There must be a lot of good in your father, Jack."

"Thank you. Lot of good in you, too."

"Thank *you*. Thank you very very much."

Joshua exclaimed, "Hey! There comes the sun right up behind the good old Green Mountains of Vermont!"

Bonesteel leaned back happy.

4

ON THE LIGHTEST of airs the *South Wind* ghosted along the western shore of Valcour Island where, silhouetted against the eastern sky, tall pines were etched in grays and blacks. In the forest beyond, the companions heard the cries of a multitude of birds, cut sharply by the harsh caw of crows. A great flight of wild pigeons arose and wheeled toward the mainland. Far in the interior a fox twanged his unpleasant bark. Near at hand, on the water, rhythmic shadows wove and broke. A great bass, hungry and full of spunk, leaped clear, snapped at a shadfly, shook his tail, and fell back with a splash. Farther down the channel, between the island and the mainland, sea gulls were beginning their day's fishing.

"Everything in nature feeds on everything else," Bonesteel said. "But that's the way God made 'em. So that's good. But God didn't make man to destroy man. That's bad."

Joshua exclaimed, "I'm getting hungry. Let's have fish for breakfast."

Bonesteel saw that both boys were laughing at him for the surprise that must have been on his face. So he had to laugh too.

"Right. Lovely as this place is, we can't eat it. We'll pull in by that ledge yonder, and fish it will be."

"I'll catch 'em," Joshua offered.

"And I build the fire," Jack said. "You hungry too, Mister Teach?"

"I could eat a horse. . . . All this beauty is to start the day right with. And no more superstitions. No more Carcajou, either."

"You think many good things."

"That's the way I try to live, Jack."

Jack looked eastward as though trying to reach Smuggler Bay. "Maybe me too be like you."

Bonesteel asked, "Do you remember the wrestling match?"

"Most certainly."

"I was afraid it wouldn't turn out right. Did you know that?"

Jack smiled. "Yes. I knew."

"Well, it did. Better than I hoped."

Bonesteel worked the *South Wind* to the small sand beach close to the ledge. Jack leaped ashore and started gathering cedar driftwood for a quick fire, and dry hardwood for the fire-hole beans. Joshua mounted the ledge and baited up. As soon as the first fine perch came wriggling out of the water, Bonesteel was cleaning it. Presently there were a dozen perch sizzling in the big iron skillet; and Jack was digging the hole, building a fire in it, and preparing the blackened beanpot which would go in on a deep bed of coals.

Into the beanpot Jack poured molasses and a small amount of mustard and salt, followed by a chunk of salt pork. The beans had been soaking since the night before, and the whole business would be "integrated," as Bonesteel put it, in about eight hours. The boys laughed about the "integrated" beans, and looked forward to eating them with hot buttered cornbread.

"Fish about done," Bonesteel shouted. "We'll take a quick swim. Then we'll eat."

Jack rolled several rocks into the fire hole, and then stripped. "Last one in is a big—"

"Carcajou!" Joshua shouted from the boat.

Bonesteel roared with laughter as both boys hit the water at the same time. Then he shouted, "Make way for the Carcajou!" And he too plunged in.

After breakfast they went to sleep in the shade on the sand beach. The *South Wind* was drawn up until her keel just kissed the sand bottom. And Little Loup was on guard. With the dog and Bonesteel's gun they would be as safe as an army with pickets, so Bonesteel had said.

It was afternoon when the adventurers awoke refreshed.

While Bonesteel turned out a batch of golden cornbread, which Little Loup pronounced good, Jack raked away the earth and rolled out the stones.

Bonesteel looked at the mouth-watering beanpot and made a suggestion. "Let's take this stuff aboard and set sail. It looks like it might rain. We'll eat aboard and head for the Ausable." He looked out at the channel. "Ought to make good time. Camp in about an hour."

It was quickly agreed. But as they pulled away from shore, Little Loup leaped upon the cabin, looked back toward the island, and set up a terrific barking.

"Did we leave something?" Bonesteel asked.

They heard somebody crashing through the woods near the shore. A voice shouted, "Head him off! We got the nigra now!"

A terror-stricken Negro stumbled from the woods. His eyes were protruding, his chest was heaving, his mouth was wide, gasping for breath. He turned to put up his last desperate fight for freedom. Bonesteel snatched his gun and put the helm over to bring the *South Wind* back to the ledge.

"Here! Over here!" he shouted. Then he muttered, "He may be a runaway. But I'll take that chance."

The Negro staggered into the water, and made a feeble effort to thrash his way to the boat.

"Here's your chance to do some good too, Jack. Help him," Bonesteel said.

Presently Jack was pushing, and Joshua was pulling, the half-dead fugitive over the gunwale into the boat, where he lay on the cockpit floor, heaving and groaning.

"Now, Jack, take the helm and get us out of here, because I think I know what's going to happen next." Gun in hand, Bonesteel glared back at the shoreline.

Sure enough. Two figures burst from the woods. The

first was a sharp-faced, sallow-complexioned individual with a large glittering earring hanging from one ear. The other was an ugly, meaty person with a great mop of fiery red hair.

"There's your Carcajou. The red one," Bonesteel said. "But who's the first one?"

"Him they call Laroque," Jack replied.

"So that's Laroque, eh? My, my, hasn't he come down in the world, though? Now watch this, Jack." Bonesteel raised his gun and shouted, "All right, you two. Stand right where you are!"

The *South Wind* was traveling fast now. But Bonesteel held his gun so steady the two rascals could only stand still with their mouths open and their guns useless at their sides.

Jack rasped, "Shoot the Carcajou!"

"Sorry, Jack. You know how the gun is loaded. It wouldn't carry that far even if I had taken time to prime it. All I can do is bluff."

When Bonesteel did lower his gun the distance was great. The two slavers scampered back into the woods. The shots they fired at Bonesteel went wide.

"That's that," Bonesteel said. "Now let's have a look at our man."

The poor Negro lay sprawled upon his back just as he had fallen. The fear was gone somewhat from his eyes, but Bonesteel saw that he was still breathing heavily.

"All right. You're safe now. They shot at you. By any chance did they hit you?"

"No sir."

"That's good. If you feel like it you might tell us your name."

"Amos Lash, sir."

"What? Why, I know you. You're a freedman. You have a farm down on the west shore."

"Yes sir."

"When did this happen?"

"Three days ago."

"Your wife?" Bonesteel asked gently.

Great sobs burst from the wretched Negro. He looked up helplessly. Bonesteel nodded and pressed his lips into a hard line. "I thought so."

Amos Lash did not try to suppress his sobs. "She was bad sick. The Carcajou throwed her into the lake."

Bonesteel's temper burst out. "That red Carcajou was going to sell this man back into slavery, the murdering, thieving devil. He was going to sell his wife too. But she was sick. Nobody would want her, and he didn't want to bother. He couldn't let her live and tell about him. So he murdered her."

Jack's eyes rolled white. "I told you, Mister Teach."

Bonesteel jerked around and glared back at the island. He snatched out the buckshot pouch. "But he's not a ghost. You'll see. I'm loading buckshot, boy."

They were now clearing the south end of Valcour Island. Bonesteel was so angry he didn't know he had drawn his lips back from his teeth in such a savage expression that Joshua hesitated twice before speaking.

Finally Joshua was able to say, "The Carcajou will follow us in the *Black Sloop*."

39

Bonesteel snapped, "I want him to. . . . Close-haul between Valcour and Garden Island, Jack. And be quick about it!"

Amos leaped up. "Don't ye do it. Please, sir. They's five of them."

"So there are five of them!" Bonesteel barked.

"Yes sir. The two you saw, the German cook, a British officer, and the man they call the Pilot."

A quick glance told Bonesteel Jack didn't move a muscle at the mention of his father. Bonesteel looked back at Amos and said quickly, "A British officer. By heaven, what next?"

"Yes sir, yes sir. But don't ye do it. They'll gun ye."

Reluctantly Bonesteel saw Amos was right. "Put back, Jack. We'll head back to Plattsburg and report this to the General."

But Jack's face was blank. He held his course.

"Put about, Jack. We'll head back to town!"

Jack mumbled, "Do no good. He catch us in the channel."

"Then south! What's the matter with you? Are you daft, boy?"

Bonesteel sensed that Jack was almost paralyzed with fear. But this time he seemed about to obey.

Joshua pointed and said, "There's the *Black Sloop.* There's the Carcajou."

Amos dropped to his knees.

Bonesteel saw that the *South Wind* was cut off, for while she still had Valcour's high cliffs to windward the

Black Sloop was boiling along beyond the island on the strong north wind.

"Anything we can do?" Joshua asked.

"Pray, boy, pray. Tell God we've got the Carcajou on our trail." Bonesteel laughed bitterly. "We ought to have Matthew Standish here. He'd pray that red devil right off the lake." He turned to Jack. "You're doing fine, Jack. Steady as you go."

Now the people on the *Black Sloop* were easy to see. Bonesteel counted them. "One, two, three. I don't see your father, Jack. And I don't see that British officer. The helmsman will be too busy. That leaves only two to deal with."

"Laroque at the helm," Jack said mechanically.

"Amos, look alive now. Who's that big stupid-looking oaf standing by the Carcajou?"

"That's—that's the German cook."

"All right. Buck up. It's that cook and the Carcajou we have to deal with. The odds aren't so bad. Keep praying."

"Us is," Amos chattered.

The *Black Sloop* was rapidly closing the gap. Bonesteel saw that already the Carcajou was leaning far out over the rail and was pointing his two pistols at him. But now that Bonesteel was in it he was not in the least daunted. He leveled his gun at the Carcajou.

The Carcajou's jaw snapped up and down. "You stole my nigger! Fetch him over here, or I'll blast ye!"

Bonesteel shouted back, "I'll swap shots with you,

Carcajou. I've got buckshot here." Out of the corner of his mouth he said again, "Keep on praying."

Both boats were now sailing in a gusty wind. Something happened—something that doesn't happen often in a whole lifetime of good boat handling. Bonesteel told Standish later that it must have been the praying that did it.

The *Black Sloop's* boom began to lift. Up and up the mast it crept. Bonesteel and his friends saw it, but nobody on the *Black Sloop* did, so determined were they to recapture Amos Lash.

Bonesteel shouted, "Broad off, Jack!"

The *Black Sloop* altered her course to follow. Her boom slid away up.

"A goosewing! The Carcajou's got a goosewing!" Bonesteel shouted. Then, thinking of his own mainsail, he called, "Watch her, Jack, boy."

Now the Carcajou felt the trouble. He spun around and looked up. So infuriated was he at what he saw, and by the laughter from the *South Wind* that he must have heard, that he lost his head completely and fired both pistols at his own crazily billowing mainsail. And the cook, suddenly excited, discharged his gun harmlessly. The *Black Sloop* lurched. The cook dropped his gun overboard. The Carcajou fell to his knees and presented to Bonesteel the best possible target.

"Now!" Bonesteel breathed triumphantly. He squeezed the trigger.

The Carcajou screamed, seized at the place where he

42

was wounded, charged across the deck, and plunged into the lake on the other side.

Laroque fumbled at the helm. The boom slid down. He fumbled again. The boom jibed and snapped off—completely splintered and broken.

The *Black Sloop* was totally disabled, and her captain was blubbering in the cold water of the lake of which he thought he was the master.

The *South Wind* sailed away.

Jack was trying to say something. There was a completely un-Indian-like expression on his face. At last Bonesteel stopped laughing to listen to him.

In amazement Jack whispered, "Rock salt, pig bristles, and buckshot. . . . The Carcajou!"

5

A SLIGHT misty rain had begun to fall. The *South Wind* sailed into the wetness.

Bonesteel sat cleaning his gun. Now and again he looked up. There sat Amos Lash on the windward side of the boat, his arms hooked backward over the coaming, his body yielding like a dead thing, his eyes fixed. Bonesteel's heart twisted to see it. And there sat Jack thinking of his father, Bonesteel knew.

Bonesteel threaded a greased rag through the ramrod's eye and passed it down the long barrel. He too was thinking about Jack's father. He passed the greased rag down the barrel again. . . . And for the moment, there was this British officer in the picture, too.

What was a British officer doing with the *Black Sloop* Gang? With the Carcajou? With Jack's father?

Bonesteel started wiping down the outside of the gun.

Was the Carcajou trading with the enemy? There was a lot of that going on.

But would that explain why a British officer, in uniform, would risk coming so far south of the frontier? . . . There might be something more to all this.

44

Bonesteel heard Joshua speaking to him. He looked up. "What is it, Joshua?"

"Amos needs food, Mr. Bonesteel. . . . I guess we're all hungry. I know I am."

Bonesteel threw a glance at the Negro's face. How deep-lined and weary it was. "May I be smitten! Of course he does! Give him a big plate of those beans—a big plate. Sure, let's all eat."

Joshua dove into the small cabin and brought out the forgotten beanpot and cornbread.

Amos turned away. "I ain't hungry, son. I really ain't."

Joshua grinned and pushed a heaping plate into Amos' hands. "Aw, come on, Amos. Try it—for us."

Amos began to eat listlessly, just to be polite. But as his starving body awakened he ate faster.

Presently Bonesteel exclaimed, "Man alive, you're hollow!"

Between mouthfuls Amos mumbled back at him, "Hain't ate much in three days. . . . Couldn't have ate that cook's slop if I'd wanted to."

"We haven't eaten since morning, and we're hungry. You must be starved."

Amos looked at his plate. "Give me some more them beans, please, boy." And when his plate was filled to heaping he started to say something. "I guess I"—but he couldn't finish because he was eating again.

At last everybody was filled up, even Amos. They couldn't have eaten another "integrated" bean. "Hats off to Jack's beans," Bonesteel exclaimed.

45

Then Bonesteel was serious. "Amos, you said a British officer is with the gang on the island. Can you tell me anything about him?"

Amos's eyes were alert. "Yes sir—yes sir. I can. I forget till now, I was so took with my misery."

"Good. It's very important."

"He's a navy man—a tall one, tall and haughty-like."

"Tall and haughty, eh?"

"He'd come over to where I was tied up, put his arms behind him, lean over, stick his big long thin nose in my face—and just peer at me."

Bonesteel nodded.

Amos continued. "Big long thin nose, like a hawk."

"Well, wouldn't he say anything?"

Amos shook his head. "Nope. Seems like he was all braced up inside his head, tight and satisfied. . . . Didn't say nothing."

"Well—" Bonesteel had another question, but Amos interrupted him.

"Warn't no kindness in him. No sir. No kindness."

"That's about what I was going to ask." Then Bonesteel wrinkled his forehead, trying to remember something. "Long thin nose. . . . Long thin nose."

Amos interrupted him again. "Yes sir!" he said emphatically.

"Ought to be easy to pick him out again."

"Oh, yes sir. And he played a little flute. Seems like he need to every now and then. Played good, too."

"He did?"

"He'd get talking haughtier and haughtier with the

46

Carcajou, and his nose would begin to quiver like the wind puffing a sail. Then he'd go off and play on that little flute to calm hisself down."

Now Bonesteel was alert. "What did he talk to the Carcajou about?"

"Oh, a lot of things."

"Anything about Plattsburg, Burlington, about Macomb, Macdonough, the British?"

Amos thrust up his hand. "I got it. He said that even though Macdonough was on the lake now with his fleet, they was going to fool Macdonough anyhow."

"Fool him?"

"He said they was a-coming to Valcour Island and he would have some information for them."

"Let me get this straight. Who is coming to Valcour Island?"

"The British fleet. The same British fleet that come down the lake last April."

"And who would have information for this British fleet?"

Amos scrubbed a hand over his ebony face. "Hook Nose would. That's what they call that British officer behind his back."

"I see. Hook Nose, eh? . . . Now, who is this Hook Nose going to get this information from?"

"From the Carcajou. And *he* is getting it from somebody who is coming to Valcour Island from Plattsburg. The Carcajou said that that somebody will do anything for money."

Bonesteel slapped his fist into his palm. "A spy system

47

working right through the *Black Sloop* Gang to the British fleet." He saw Jack wanted to speak. And he suddenly remembered.

"Did you see my father, Mr. Lash?" Jack asked. "He is not a spy."

"I don't know your pappy, son."

Jack's face was wooden. "He is the one they call the Pilot."

"Oh, the one the Carcajou was always getting drunk." Then Amos was ashamed. "I's sorry I said that."

Bonesteel saw that he must comfort Jack with a smile, and that made Amos more uneasy.

But then Amos slapped his forehead. "Wait a minute. The Pilot. Oh me, oh my. That's why the Carcajou keep trying to get him drunker."

"Why, Amos?" Bonesteel asked.

"That Pilot he vowed he wouldn't not pilot the *Vermont*. That old Carcajou said he would when he was drunk enough. But that Pilot he got mad like a blue jay and said he wouldn't not nohow!"

Bonesteel sat up straight. "Do you mean the *Vermont*, the steamboat?"

"Yes sir. The *Vermont* steamboat at Burlington. That's why the British fleet's hanging around. To swipe the steamboat."

"Why that's the first steamboat on Lake Champlain. And the British want to get it. Go on, Amos."

"That about all. The British fleet is a-waiting over there by Providence Island to catch the *Vermont* when she comes snorting by."

48

Bonesteel shook his head in disbelief. "This war. So they want the *Vermont*. I'm certain that is more than mischief. . . . And while they're doing that this Hook Nose will get some information from the Carcajou, who will get it from somebody who will do anything for money. Hook Nose will pass it on to the British fleet. *And* while he's doing *that* Jack's father will refuse to pilot the *Vermont*." Bonesteel wagged his head again and looked at Jack. "There's one *man* on that Island, isn't there, Jack, boy?"

Jack lifted his chin proudly. His smile was cold and bitter.

Joshua said, "Our cruise is sort of spreading out. Isn't it?"

"You're quite right there."

"Then I say we go to Burlington and warn the *Vermont*."

"We've got to," Bonesteel said.

Amos said, "I be glad to go."

Bonesteel turned to Jack. "What do you say, Jack?"

Jack replied, "For my father I go, though he does not need my help."

Bonesteel was on the verge of telling Jack that warning the *Vermont* might lead to more trouble for his father than anybody could help him out of. But instead, he put his hand on Jack's shoulder and smiled. "Of course, we all know how well your father can take care of himself."

Jack smiled back.

49

6

THE MISTY RAIN had stopped, and so in spite of the urgency Bonesteel had shouted happily, "Let her sail!"

Now the *South Wind* was flying toward Burlington across the miles of open water of the broad lake. It was close-hauled and fast all the way.

Just before the sun plunged down behind the violet Adirondacks far to the west the *South Wind* spied the *Vermont* anchored under the guns of the General's batteries up on the bluff beyond the beach.

Bonesteel shouted, "There she is. Ahoy the *Vermont*! Will you take our line? We have information for your captain."

A head and shoulders appeared above the rail. "I'm the captain, and it's a nice evening. What's this about information?"

"Yes sir. It is a nice evening, since it is your good fortune that we find you in port." Bonesteel turned to the boys. "Wake Amos up. Snug things down and we'll all go aboard."

"You sound serious," the Captain said.

Bonesteel started up the ladder. "I am. We're from

Plattsburg, Captain. I'm Hosea Bonesteel, schoolmaster. And I'm mighty glad I found you here."

"You found me here because my engine has busted down again." Sounds of metal striking metal came from the engine hatch. The Captain took Bonesteel's arm and propelled him toward the sounds.

"We'll drive sin out of those bearing wedges this time. I'm two hours late already."

Bonesteel looked down at the simple twenty-horsepower engine and was tempted to ask how it worked. Instead he said, "Now, how about what I came to tell you?"

"All right. I've got time. I guess I've got a lot of time."

"In private, Captain."

The Captain shot Bonesteel a quick glance, and started toward the large deckhouse at the stern. "There's only one person in here."

"Very private."

"It's General Macomb. Is he all right?"

"This is good luck. He's one of the two other men hereabouts who should hear this too, besides yourself."

The Captain's hand stopped in mid-air. "Who's the other one?"

"Commodore Macdonough."

"Hum. . . . Sounds real serious, young man."

"It is."

At that moment Amos and the boys joined them.

A little surprised, the Captain looked at the Negro. But then he smiled his friendliest smile. "What are you doing here, Amos?"

"He's part of the story," Bonesteel said.

Deeply puzzled now, the Captain swung open the door. As Bonesteel swept his eyes around the interior he realized he was a little pleased with the mystery he was creating, even to the way his three friends huddled close behind him. He knew he ought not to be pleased. But he was.

Around the walls were built-in double-decker bunks. From a carline overhead swung a smelly whale-oil ship lantern. Beneath it, fastened to the floor, was a heavy table flanked by benches. And in the center of the feeble pool of light sat the ruddy-complexioned young Brigadier General Macomb mumbling at papers which he had spread on the table before him.

Without looking up the General started talking, and Bonesteel hadn't heard very much before he was mighty glad they had come.

"That's the way it is, Captain. We need your *Vermont*. You'll be supply ship to Commodore Macdonough's fleet. I'll use you some. When I need you I'll let him know, and he'll pass the word." The General slapped his hand hard on the table. "We'll need every hull afloat. We're —well, we're desperate. I guess you know that. We've got to improvise."

The Captain coughed, and suddenly Bonesteel felt the General's penetrating stare. Then as quickly a warm light came into the General's face.

He leaped up. "Oh ho! The fighting schoolmaster and the young men who—how are you, Bonesteel, and Joshua Benson and Muskrat Jack?"

When the whole story had been told, the Captain puffed out his cheeks. "Now that's something. If that old engine of mine hadn't broken down, where'd I be now? And where would you and the Commodore be, General?"

"If you weren't dead, you'd be working for the King of England. But I think you'd be dead. . . . And we? . . . A bad setback when we could least afford it." The General scrubbed his fingers through his curly brown hair. "They're getting high and mighty sassy. Aren't they?"

Bonesteel caught fire from the General. "That they are, sir! That they are!"

The General lifted his eyes. Bonesteel saw how fierce they could be. He blinked when the General slapped the table, and exclaimed, "I'd like to catch that picaroon of a Carcajou! I'd hang him! Eh—Amos and Jack? That's just a little something extra I'd like to do while I'm here. But I'm so busy and shorthanded I can't even do that!"

Bonesteel looked sidewise at Jack. Jack didn't move a muscle.

Then the General seemed to bite down on a decision. "I'll tell you something, though. Just to show you how critical everything is, and how everything may just tie together."

The *Vermont* rocked gently in the evening wind. The ship's lantern angled slowly back and forth. Bonesteel felt the suspense.

The General said, "You'll be the first around here to know about this. It's damnable news for our people to take right now. . . . Napoleon has abdicated."

53

Bonesteel stared at him.

"I see you don't know what that means?"

Bonesteel shook his head.

"It means: no more Napoleon; no more British armies needed in Europe."

"You mean—?"

"Right you are, schoolmaster. They'll all come over here, thousands of them, trained and tough, Wellington's regiments—fresh from licking old Boney, the smartest of them all. . . . And my guess is that most of them will come right over here into this valley." The General drew in a quick breath. "But don't worry. We'll be ready for them, won't we, schoolmaster? I remember that schoolyard fight."

Bonesteel nodded.

"And in the meantime, there will be work for all—for us *and* the British. That's why they wanted to get the *Vermont*. They think they need it as much as we do."

The Captain broke in. "Looks to me as though we're going to see some hustling this summer. Some folks had just about given up hope that anything was going to be done. And some folks have gone to trading right out in the open with Canada. Why, right here in Vermont—"

The General interrupted. "Some of them are just radicals, but some others are just plain skunks. But just wait until the invasion starts. They'll get patriotic in a hurry. You'll see. . . . But as you say, we'll see some hustling this summer. And some people around here are going to get shot at before snow flies—by the British, I mean."

Bonesteel looked around, but especially at Jack. He must say what was uppermost in his mind. "About the war in this valley there's no doubt. But about the gang: There's one man in that gang who is different. He is Jack's father, the Pilot."

The General smiled, and Bonesteel heard a gentler note in his voice. "Bonesteel, I'm a soldier; you're a schoolmaster. I see this war as it affects the whole country. Well, I suppose you do too. But you also see it as it affects Jack, here." He got up and started pacing back and forth. "Perhaps in the long view your work is more important than mine. But it is also true that without men like me you might not have any work. So try to see it my way." The General turned and smiled. "What is it Jack calls you?"

"He calls me Mister Teach, sir."

"It's an honor. With your permission I shall call you that, myself."

As they started to leave the ship the Captain said, "Amos, what are you going to do now?"

Bonesteel interrupted, "I'd planned to take him to Plattsburg with us, Captain. We can find him work there."

The Captain stroked his chin. "Well, now, Amos will be safe with me, here. I'll give him work. There'll be plenty of that right soon—what with the *Vermont* attached to the fleet."

It touched Bonesteel's heart to see Amos look out into the night toward the New York shore where he and his wife had been so happy only a few days before.

"That's the thing to do, Amos," he said gently.

Amos's eyes came back. "If you all ever needs help, Mister Teach, sir, just you call on Amos Lash. He'll be right here on this steamboat, waiting for you."

Very late that night the *South Wind* was beating back through the channel between Valcour and the New York shore. When Bonesteel was well under the deeper shadows of the mainland Jack suddenly pointed lakeward. "Look," he whispered hoarsely. "Look!"

A strange sloop was making toward them. Bonesteel peered apprehensively. "Guns!" he whispered back. Then as the sinister sloop came up into the wind and faint but crisp orders came to him, he gasped, "They're British!"

"Do they see us?" Joshua asked.

"Don't think so. But what are they doing over here in these waters? Pull up the centerboard. We'll drift inshore."

Little Loup growled.

Bonesteel whispered sharply, "Keep him quiet, Jack."

Jack seized the dog's muzzle. "You be quiet, you!"

"Good dog," Bonesteel whispered, relieved. "Now you boys get overside and hold on. We'll drift. When you get a good foothold on the bottom, hold her off the wind a whisker. Then the sail won't flap. In close to shore they won't see us, I hope. . . . Sand bottom here."

The water was cold. The boys gasped.

"Sh-h!"

"Bottom," Jack whispered.

"Ride her in until you're waist-deep. Then do as I said."

Bonesteel was watching the enemy sloop. Someone was pulling in on a line towing a rowboat. A short fat man was preparing to get into it. A tall officer with a long sharp face appeared in a little pool of guarded light. The officer had a large nose. He spoke in a low tense voice.

He said, "Don't forget, Potts, information is what we're paying you for. Information and beef. We'll buy all the information and beef you can deliver."

Bonesteel gasped. He remembered what Amos had told them. But he had not mentioned beef. Apparently the British had bargained further with this Potts for beef.

The officer spoke again. "Get in. I'll cast you loose."

"Hook Nose!" Bonesteel whispered. He seized his gun, but laid it down again.

Potts hesitated and stepped back into the light. "What happens if the Carcajou dies?" he asked in a quavering voice.

"Then you deal directly with me. But he won't die. That fantastic schoolmaster's bullet will give him a limp as long as he lives. But it won't kill him."

"I—I'm in this deeper than I had planned," Potts wailed.

"You're in this up to your neck, Potts. If you don't like that, you should have thought of it before. Now shove off. This is a lee shore for us. We've got to get out of here."

Presently Potts was rowing a brief but erratic course for shore.

When it was safe, Bonesteel said, "Get in, boys. I forgot all about you."

Jack leaped overside and squatted in the cockpit. "Mister Teach," he chattered, "do you know who that Hook Nose is?"

Bonesteel dropped the centerboard and put the *South Wind* on the larboard tack. "No. Who?"

"He's the man you fought with in the schoolyard."

Bonesteel struck the coaming. "Of course he is!"

7

I T WAS WHILE Bonesteel was pacing back and forth in his room, and beating his fist against his forehead, that somebody knocked on his door. He opened it. Jack was standing there.

Bonesteel would have preferred not to see Jack just then, but he had to say, "Oh, come in, Jack. I was just thinking about you."

Jack crossed the room and sat down cross-legged upon the floor against the wall. "We talk, Mister Teach?"

"All right. I guess we'd better."

"I think Potts is a spy. And I think that if he is a spy, my father is in great danger."

Bonesteel jammed his hands into his pockets and walked to the window. "That's just it. But if Potts is a spy, you know what I've got to do about it." He heard Jack get up. He turned around. Jack was going toward the door. "No, no. I don't mean that yet. I just mean that I don't know whether he is or not. And although I don't like him—well. Come back and sit down, Jack. Please."

"I sit down."

"Have you got any ideas?"

Bonesteel saw Jack studying his face, and he felt the great distance between the Indian and the white man. But when Jack spoke, it was just a boy, any boy, clinging to a friend. "You have done much for me, Mister Teach. You have stood against Mr. Wall for me. I know that. You have say good things about my father when they were hard to say. I know that too. You have attacked the Carcajou—for Amos Lash, yes, but for me too. Why you do all these things?"

"Because I don't like to see people get pushed around, I guess."

"But for me, Mister Teach?"

Bonesteel looked out the window again. "All right, Jack. Let's say there are some young fellows in this unkind world who are worth it. I think you are one of them."

"Thank you. I not forget that. Now I ask you do one more thing."

"What?" Somehow Bonesteel dreaded what was coming.

"If they find out Potts is a spy they will kill the gang. Is that not correct?"

Bonesteel nodded.

"Then will you help me look for my father one week on the lake in the *South Wind?*"

Bonesteel started cracking his knuckles. "I don't know whether Potts is a spy or not, do I?" Then he got angry with himself. "What am I saying? Hook Nose was there, and so was a British sloop-of-war."

Jack stood stiff, his face an unfathomable Indian mask.

60

"If we do not find my father, all right. Then you do what you think best about Potts."

Bonesteel blew out his cheeks. "All right, Jack. I'll do it for you. Seems as though I couldn't do anything else. But God forgive me if I'm doing wrong."

It was a fruitless week, and before it was over Bonesteel knew they weren't going to succeed. Meanwhile he felt suspended between the past that had happened, and the unknown future. He wanted to hurry up and get into the future and control it before it controlled him. But he would have to search the week out. He had promised.

From Valcour north to the border they searched. They got so close they could see the British galleys hovering off the entrance to the Richelieu River.

Then Bonesteel heard that the *Black Sloop* was in the Richelieu, in enemy territory, and wouldn't come out for some time. He sailed the *South Wind* back to Plattsburg, where Jack told Joshua all that had happened.

While Jack was telling Joshua, Bonesteel was hearing things about the war. British soldiers and Canadian militia were massing at the frontier. At one place there were already 3600. At three other important places they were beefing up the garrisons to fighting strength, and were building a naval base at Isle aux Noix in the Richelieu. Already they had a fleet well along there, and they were building a great flagship, the *Confiance,* bigger and heavier than Macdonough's flagship, the *Saratoga.* . . . The Americans were getting set too, if Bonesteel could believe all he heard. There were 1400 men encamped at one frontier town and 800 at another, while just north of Plattsburg 1200 more were digging in. In Plattsburg, itself, army engineers were surveying for more forts. On the lake Captain Macdonough was moving his fleet to King's Bay up near the border where he would sound the bottom for a good battle area.

It was clear that Plattsburg was going to get it. But Bonesteel hadn't yet made up his mind about Potts. He felt guilty. But everything stayed in suspense—waiting.

"I've got to get at something while I'm trying to decide," he told Jack.

Jack's reply was sullen. "You go ahead, Mister Teach. Tell about Potts. I do not find my father. I got nobody. This not my wars. Me, I'm Indian."

"Now wait a minute, Jack. You've got me. And this can be just as much your country as it is mine."

Jack shrugged his shoulders. "Me, I go away. Huh!"

"Do you know why this country can be just as much yours?"

"Me, I don't care."

"Because it stands for the best that you and I believe in. Don't let this problem about your father blind you. Look, Jack. I've made sacrifices for you. Now it's your turn to make some for me. I'm sure your Indian blood will tell you this is a debt of honor."

"Indian always pay debt of honor."

"All right then. Come with me out to Fort Izard on Cumberland Head. They need men desperately to help with the building. And *we* need to be a part of something bigger than our personal problems are, bigger than we are."

Jack drew himself up proudly. "For *you* I come."

Bonesteel grinned. "Good boy, Jack. . . . And Jack—?"

Jack lifted his chin to show that he was listening.

"I know the Indian and the white man don't always think alike. So I'm proud of you for your decision. And so I tell you I'm not forgetting your father. You can see that, can't you?"

On the way to Cumberland Head Bonesteel observed closely the hundreds of men all about, preparing for what they were sure would be an invasion. Army regulars he saw, and militia, and volunteers. They were felling the forest so that cannoneers and soldiers could look northward and have a clear field of fire.

At Fort Izard it was the same, and Bonesteel and Jack went immediately to work.

Swinging an axe, handling a shovel, working behind oxen snagging out boulders and stumps—Bonesteel knew that in time his head would clear enough so he could decide what he ought to do. Even when they had to stand in thick smudge smoke, of an evening, to escape the black flies and mosquitoes, and sleep with heads under blankets, Bonesteel was willing to wait for the answer. . . . And Jack worked well, and seemed to be strangely content.

Bonesteel knew the value of hard physical work, and of being with men who were also working hard. There was something about it that healed a man's indecision. He looked around.

63

There was a strong brotherhood here. He and Jack were drawn into it. Oh, it was true the men fought each other sometimes. That was only natural. Tempers were quick. But the next moment they were strangely good to one another, in a rough sort of way. And Bonesteel, seeking his answer, would say, "See, Jack?"

Often a man would stop working, stand up straight, and look north—though he couldn't see much beyond the dirt embankment, or beyond the woods, or very far down the lake. His neighbor would tell him, "Take it easy, friend. Just take it easy."

Bonesteel wanted all this to make a deep impression on Jack. He would say things to him to get him to compare these men with the *Black Sloop* Gang. Then he would watch Jack. Could Jack understand what patriotism, love of country, meant? Would Jack understand his decision about Potts when he finally made it? If it went against Jack?

Maybe I'm thinking so much with my heart that I'm all mixed up and right on the edge of trouble, Bonesteel thought. But it will come out all right. It's got to.

8

BONESTEEL pulled the light blanket from his head and looked out into the night. "Who's that?"

"It's me. Joshua."

Bonesteel sat up quickly.

"You sure are hard to wake up. What you got that blanket over your head for?"

"Mosquitoes. What are you doing here?"

"I've got bad news. Can we talk somewhere?"

Bonesteel led Joshua carefully among the sleeping men until they were quite away from the fort and anybody who could hear them.

"All right now, what's this all about?"

"It's about Potts, and my father, and Matthew Standish —and you."

"Me? That's quite a list. Haven't I got enough trouble?"

"You have. But maybe I'd better start at the beginning. Then maybe it won't seem so bad."

"Please do."

"It all started when Potts came into the store, day be-

65

fore yesterday, all dressed up in silly new clothes—Empire style, he called them; kinda Frenchy they looked to me, but expensive—and began to show off."

"What did he do?"

"Oh, he waggled himself all over the place and talked about how his clothes was imported, and then he said what he had come for."

"What was that?"

"He wanted to buy some tea, I think it was."

"Tea? I can't see anything wrong in that."

"Nor could my father, until he paid for it with a gold sovereign."

"A gold sovereign?"

"That made my father mad because he was curious where Potts got such money, and because he didn't have enough cash in the store to change it."

Bonesteel sat down on a stump and folded his arms. "All right now, Joshua, suppose you tell me everything that happened. I'll not interrupt you until you're done." And Bonesteel watched every expression on Joshua's face, as well as he could in the moonlight, until all had been told.

Then Bonesteel had unfolded his arms and said, "I think I've got it. Let me ask a few questions to put it all straight in my mind. First, you say Matthew Standish was there too, and that when Potts had gone both your father and Matthew agreed that Potts with that much money and those new clothes was very suspicious? And that Matthew then said the whole business would bear looking into?"

"Yes."

"And you said that Potts talked against what I was doing for Jack? Said I might better give my time to the 'worthy sons of the community,' rather than to half-breed trash?"

"Yes."

"Looks as though the Carcajou told Potts about Amos Lash, and Potts is afraid now that somehow or other we'll find out about Potts's connection with the gang—which we have already. Doesn't it look like that to you?"

"It sure does."

"And finally, after Potts had gone, one thing led to another until your father found out about quite a bit of our cruise and what happened—without your telling him that we had definitely seen Potts?"

"Yes. And if things go on like this Matthew will run the whole story down. It will get known. You'll get in a lot of trouble, and probably the gang will end up with ropes around their necks, and that will mean Jack's father, and probably that will mean the end of Jack as far as you're concerned."

While Joshua was saying all this Bonesteel was searching his face. Suddenly he slapped his fist into his palm, and burst out laughing. "Potts got us into this and until now I haven't known what to do about it. But now I know. I can make him get us out of it!"

"How?"

"He's going to get the *Black Sloop* back for us. That's how. And what's more, we've got to get back to town tonight. And there's a problem."

Joshua said, "No it isn't. I've got the *South Wind* here. But I—"

Bonesteel cut him off. "You have? Where?"

"Down a little south of the wharf."

"Good. I'll get Jack, and we'll get going."

"I don't see what you're driving at."

Bonesteel dug his thumb playfully into Joshua's ribs. He hadn't felt so good for days. "You come along, m'boy, and you'll see. At last I've got everything figured out."

About three o'clock that morning Lycurgus Potts heard his horse, Bess, kick her stall. He leaped out of bed, seized his pistol, and dashed to the window. The moonlight was good, but he saw nothing. He stood for a time looking at the stable and the cedars near the stable. Again nothing. He went back to bed.

In the cedars Bonesteel whispered, "Go ahead, Jack. I think he's gone back to bed."

Jack crouched forward and threw a handful of gravel against Potts's window. They heard his bed squeak, and they pictured him jumping out of bed again. Bonesteel had to smile. He would have smiled more if he had actually seen Potts, pistol in hand, standing perspiring in the middle of the floor.

Jack called softly. "Mr. Potts."

"W-who's there?" from inside the house.

"It is me, Muskrat Jack. For you I have one message."

"W-who from?"

Jack went to the window, cupped his hands against the

pane, peered in, and whispered hoarsely, "A British officer."

Potts came trembling to the window. "Who did you say?"

Jack turned toward Bonesteel. Bonesteel made an emphatic gesture. Jack almost shouted to Potts, "A British officer. Something about information—and some beef."

Potts rattled the window open. "Sh! Information—and some beef? I—I don't believe you."

"He also say something about some gold for you. The officer he is back there in the cedars. You come. He say hurry. He say there are patrols in the streets."

"Oh dear, oh dear. Tell him—oh dear, money, money, money!"

"Quick, Mr. Potts. You must come just as you are."

"All right. All right."

As Potts was lowering himself from the window he felt a sharp pain in the small of his back.

"It is my knife, Potts," Jack said menacingly.

"You heathenish half-breed! What's that for?"

"To leave your pistol on the sill."

They were all standing well within the cedars. Bonesteel, fists on hips, a hard grin on his face, took pleasure in the silly desperate courage Potts was trying to display.

"What do you mean by this outrage to an honest citizen? Do you know I could have you arrested, sir?"

"You could, Potts, but I don't think you will." Bonesteel advanced threateningly.

Potts backed away. "Now, now, have a care, Bonesteel."

69

Bonesteel rubbed his hands on his thighs. "I'd like to have a care with you, Potts, because you're such a skunk. But instead, I'm going to let you do something for me."

Pott's swallow was more like a squeak. "I—I most certainly will not—I mean, what do you want me to do? If I like it, maybe I'll—"

Bonesteel held up his hand. "You're going to get word to the *Black Sloop* to return immediately. This is Monday. It must be back here on Friday, and at a place we will decide upon."

"Are you crazy? I don't know anything about the *Black Sloop*."

"No? Do you recall that a moment ago Jack spoke to you about information and gold?"

Potts's hand flew to his mouth. His eyes widened.

Bonesteel seized him by his nightshirt. "You're not even a good spy, Potts."

"Spy?" Potts squealed.

"No. You show your feelings too easily. But let me remind you of something. Not long ago a British sloop-of-war came up into the wind near the New York shore opposite Valcour. It was night, wasn't it?"

Potts licked his lips but did not answer.

"I see you do remember. It *was* night, but not so dark but what a certain Lycurgus Potts was seen aboard that sloop and *heard* talking to a British officer—the same man I fought earlier this spring in the schoolyard."

Potts gasped.

"There was something said about information and beef, wasn't there? And something about you being in this 'up to your neck'?"

Potts whispered hoarsely, "It's a lie, every bit of it!"

Bonesteel bit his words off. "I beg to differ with you, Potts, because when that interesting conversation was finished, the officer—Hook Nose, I believe they call him—pulled in the rowboat, and you got in it and rowed yourself to shore."

Potts reeled. "I—I—was a captive. Honest I was."

"No, Potts, you were a spy—a spy against your own people."

Potts's eyes shifted quickly for a way to escape. Jack and Joshua pressed him so closely that he could not.

Then Potts slumped to his knees and raised his clasped hands in supplication. "Think of my reputation, Mr. Bonesteel, sir. . . . I know I've done something I shouldn't. But the Carcajou tricked me into it. . . . I tried to get away. . . . We can fix this up, you and me. . . . If it's money—"

"Oh, get up on your feet. Get the *Black Sloop* here at some place we can agree on so I can meet it Friday night."

Potts got up, but he couldn't stop his trembling. "What if I can't?"

"If you *don't,* I'll go to Matthew Standish and tell him what I know about you. He'll no doubt go to the General. And the General will probably hang you as you deserve—unless the Carcajou gets the wind up first and deals with you personally, which wouldn't be nice. Would it?"

This set Potts to jerking violently. "If—if I do?"

Bonesteel took a deep breath. He had implicated himself too much already. But he would not promise protection. "I'll make no bargain with you, Potts. You just do what I say."

"And the boys here?"

"They'll do what I say, too."

"All right. I'll get word to the *Black Sloop* to be at Goose Pond Swamp Friday night."

Bonesteel knew about the swamp's treachery. But he would have Jack to guide him. Nevertheless, all week he had a growing conviction that Potts was going to try to trick him, perhaps using the swamp's treachery, perhaps by some other means.

Then, to complicate Bonesteel's troubles, Mr. Benson, Joshua's father, sought him out and said that as a result of a conversation with Mr. Wall he did not want Joshua to go on any more of Bonesteel's "wild cruises," as he put it.

When Bonesteel said he did not accept Mr. Wall's opinions, Mr. Benson asked, "Very well, then, would you be willing to tell me *all* that happened on your cruise?"

Bonesteel would not lie. But he wouldn't tell, either. So all he could do was stick out his jaw and say, "No, I would not!"

"Well then," Mr. Benson had replied in a kind of fretful temper, "I intend to find out some things. But in the meantime, don't take Joshua again. I'm warning you." And he had ended up by shaking his fist under Bonesteel's nose. Bonesteel was sorry. He liked Mr. Benson very much.

Altogether it was an uneasy week for Bonesteel, a week in which he had ample time to count the cost of befriending Jack. But it was also a week in which he never wavered in his determination to stick.

However, he would not be reckless. Nor would he flout Mr. Benson. To avoid any trick Potts might have in mind, and to evade Joshua, Bonesteel told Jack they would slip out of town a day earlier—on Thursday. This they did, going overland on foot—Bonesteel armed with his gun, Jack with his knife.

"We'll get your father away, Jack," Bonesteel said, as they took the north road. "Then we'll expose Potts."

Jack was walking with his head down, his face flat and expressionless, his eyes inward. "Why my father like that life with the gang, Mister Teach?"

"Maybe that's the only one he knows."

After they made a hidden camp where they could watch both the swamp and the lake, Jack circled forward to reconnoiter. He was gone until sunset. When he came back he was laughing.

"The hideout there all right, but they are not there yet."

"What's so funny about that, you young rascal?"

"Oh, that's not funny. Something else is."

"Well, what?" Bonesteel did not like secrets.

But Jack only covered his mouth with his hand. Then, because he could not stop laughing, he walked away, his shoulders shaking.

Bonesteel stood up, quite nettled, and looked northward. His eyes caught something. He pointed. "Is that what you think is so funny?"

Far out on the bay the setting sun picked out a familiar sloop making her way along outside Long Point Reef.

Jack gasped. "The Carcajou! And she is now only Thursday. No, of that I do not laugh."

"All right, forget it. . . . Potts has played his trick. Hasn't he? He hoped to get to the *Black Sloop* and warn them before we showed up."

"Yes, and have plenty of time to set a trap for us."

"In spite of Mr. Benson, I wish Joshua was here. We're going to need all the strength we can muster."

For some reason that statement made Jack smile again, but Bonesteel gave it no further thought.

They watched for an hour. Slowly the *Black Sloop* skirted south along the reef, then at last, as they knew she would, she rounded and set her course across the bay. When night closed down they lost her. But when the full orange moon arose they saw her again, anchored off the swamp.

"It is now the time to go," Jack said.

But something held Bonesteel back. "Wait a little while."

Jack raised his eyebrows. "For why?"

"Just wait, that's all. It's a hunch, Jack."

"A hunch?"

Bonesteel could only shrug his shoulders.

Then they heard it. Far back along the trail from town someone was singing quavering church tunes to the slow accompaniment of the clop-clop of a walking horse.

Bonesteel jerked his head down in a sharp nod. "It's Potts. Kick out the fire."

Lycurgus Potts came nearer, singing more lustily as it grew darker. And now they saw him through the trees.

Suddenly he reined up, looked around uneasily, sniffed the air, looked northward, saw the *Black Sloop,* and jabbed his horse into a murderous gallop. "Carcajou!" he shouted. "Oh, Carcajou!"

Bonesteel nodded to Jack. "Now it is time to go, worse luck." He picked up his gun.

But Jack put a restraining hand on Bonesteel's arm. "One moment, friend." He tipped back his head and gave the cry of the mournful owl. Off to the right the cry was answered.

"What's this?" Bonesteel wanted to know.

As though to answer his question, Joshua appeared before him.

"Well, I'll be—" Bonesteel lowered his gun to the ground.

"It is this that I laugh about," Jack was chuckling again.

"Well, I'm here," Joshua said.

Bonesteel said sharply, "Joshua, you go home."

"Nope." Joshua grinned back.

"Does your father know you're here?"

"Nope. But my aunt does."

"That's a big help."

"You'd be surprised."

Bonesteel looked from one to the other. "You two certainly have a capacity for getting me into trouble." But inwardly he couldn't deny he was pleased.

Joshua laughed. "Of course you don't have a capacity for getting us into trouble, do you, Mister Teach? There never was a schoolmaster like you."

75

"Well I hope to heaven, and I mean it, that everything comes out all right."

Jack said, "Joshua is thinking only of you, my friend."

Bonesteel's voice softened. "All right. Come on. Let's get into it." What he could possibly say to Mr. Benson later he didn't know.

They started working their way cautiously forward.

Once Jack stopped and looked back. "Friendship work both ways."

Bonesteel raised his eyebrows.

"You good friends to us. We good friends to you."

9

JACK LED THEM over whitened roots and around quicksand pools to a well-hidden spot from which they could watch the Carcajou's hideout. Gritting their teeth against the dancing clouds of biting insects they dared not slap, they settled themselves as best they could.

The gang had located on a small patch of raised ground not far from the lake. The place was illuminated by a small fire.

The yellow light and smoke from the fire, and the pale moonlight, should have made the spot interesting, Bonesteel thought, but with the few dead trees ghosting here and there, and with the eerie cedars, the place was sinister. Twisting shadows, cast by the fire and the moon, played a spooky dance over everything.

Bonesteel looked around. Off to one side the gang had upended a half of an old lugger bottom. The hulk must have washed ashore on a northeast blow, and they had sawed it in two crosswise. A wreck like that would weigh about two tons even when dried out, Bonesteel judged. But there it was, stuck up like a tombstone, its gunwales rough-boarded over except for a small opening which they had indifferently draped with a crusty old blanket.

The gang was all there, except for the German cook. The redheaded Carcajou, sallow-faced Laroque, and blubbery Potts in his sorry Empire clothes—they were squatting by the fire. Bonesteel tightened when he recognized Hook Nose, the stranger, leaning against a dead tree. Hook Nose was listening to the argument at the fire, and his fingers were fretting at the flute which he held half-raised to his lips. Jack's father, the Pilot— Bonesteel recognized him immediately—was sitting a little way off, taking no interest in anything that was going on.

Bonesteel wished the Carcajou would get up and walk about. He wanted to see if his old enemy had a limp. But the Carcajou remained seated. He was asking Potts, "Tomorrow night? All of them?"

Potts's reply was eager, like a dog expecting praise. "Maybe tonight."

The Carcajou growled, "You ain't tricking me, be ye?"

"Now now, Carcajou, you can trust me. It's them I tricked, not you."

"How?"

"I told them to meet you here tomorrow night so I would have time to warn you tonight."

"Yeah?" The Carcajou didn't seem to think too well of that.

Potts lost heart rapidly. "But maybe they'll come tonight. Bonesteel ain't so dumb."

While the Carcajou looked Potts up and down, Hook Nose's fingers moved more rapidly, and his lips parted so that his long teeth showed yellow in the firelight.

Suddenly the Carcajou seized Potts's coat front, and pulled Potts's face close to his own. "Why 'maybe they will come tonight,' Potts?"

Potts trembled violently. "B-because I smelled a campfire when I come here."

The Carcajou jumped up and looked around into the recesses of the swamp. "Why didn't you look into it, you dumbhead?"

"I-it was dark."

"Of course it was dark," the Carcajou snorted, and sat down heavily.

Hook Nose spoke sharply. "This better work, Potts."

The Carcajou showed a new suspicion. "You didn't bring that Standish with you, did you?"

"No, no! I'm honest."

Hook Nose spoke rapidly. "But you brought me back into this forsaken country with a false message. You didn't have any information for me."

Potts wailed, "I had to get you here somehow, or Bonesteel would have reported me—us."

Laroque spoke up. His voice seemed to Bonesteel to be as smooth as grease. "Potts he speak the truth, gentlemen."

"But that campfire!" The Carcajou jumped up again. "Why didn't you look into it?" He reached down and jerked Potts to his feet. "Did you go and tell that Standish where I be?" He slapped Potts hard across the mouth. "Or that Mr. Benson, maybe"—he slapped again —"or Macomb?"

Potts twisted loose and started to run. Laroque seized

79

him from behind and pinned his arms. The Carcajou slapped him again.

Crazed with fright, Potts kicked out at the Carcajou's shins. "No! No! I didn't!"

"Kick me, will ye? Why you squirming little sniveler, I oughta gouge yer eyes out." He raised his dirty thumbnails to Potts's eyes. Potts screamed in terror.

Bonesteel closed his eyes and lowered his head, and was aware that he was uttering a prayer for poor Potts.

Hook Nose barked, "Hold it, Carcajou!"

Bonesteel looked up to see the Carcajou breathing heavily, backing away.

Hook Nose continued. "You are working for us now, Potts. Any idea you may have had that you are on some kind of a romantic adventure should be dispelled by what has just now happened to you."

The Carcajou thrust his face close. "Yeah. If ye squeal on us, *we* will hang you—after we've played with ye a bit. I'll give ye a slight taste." With that the Carcajou suddenly pressed his thumbnails into Potts's face and drew them down, opening long gashes. "Just to show ye I could."

Laroque laughed and dropped the screaming Potts to the ground. "I think our Mr. Potts will always tell us the truth," he said.

In the shadows Bonesteel whispered in Jack's ear. "So that's a sample."

Jack replied, "You wait. There's more. I know them."

"Whew!" Bonesteel breathed cautiously.

Now Hook Nose raised his flute. The tune he began was at first moody and slow, but soon it picked up, sprightly and fast. Laroque began to strut about and to boast in his native French tongue. Laughing, watching him, the Carcajou stood with hands on hips, and flopping his red mop of hair back and forth in time with the music. Hook Nose made the music more exciting. Jack's father looked up, then became interested in the ground again.

Bonesteel whispered in Jack's ear, "Is this the kind of thing you lived with?"

"But yes. You watch now. Something happen soon. Always does."

Into the midst of all this the German cook entered from one of the dark tunnels of foliage. He was bending his expressionless face over something he was crushing senselessly in his big hands. He bumped into Laroque. Laroque, excited, called him a name, and shoved him. The cook growled back stupidly.

Laroque shouted, "If you must kill that animal, then kill it. You beast of a beast!"

The cook, nearsighted, looked up and growled again. The Carcajou laughed at all this. Hook Nose added an extra little trill to his notes. Laroque, stung, lashed out at the cook, struck the animal from his hands, and jumped upon it, killing it instantly. The moonlight reflected from the cook's cold eyes.

"Pig!" Laroque screamed. He spat in the cook's face.

The cook dove at the fire and seized a stick of burning hardwood. He roared back, "Swill of Paris!"

Laroque snatched out his stiletto and started circling

the big German. Keeping his blinking watery eyes on Laroque's face, the cook lumbered slowly around in his tracks.

Laroque lunged, but the distance was too great.

Leaping forward and grunting like a woodchopper, the cook aimed a swishing blow at Laroque's legs. The blow was high and short, but it did open a burning gash on Laroque's thigh.

Before the cook could recover, Laroque licked out his knife and laid the flesh open on the cook's forearm.

The Carcajou jerked out his pistols and fired a shot past Laroque's head. "Leave off," he bellowed. "Drop yer sticker."

Laroque threw his stiletto on the ground, drew back his lips, and stalked off into the swamp.

For a long moment Bonesteel, Jack, and Joshua lay very still, stunned by such senseless savagery. During that moment Potts got up, staggered a little way off, sat himself down on a log, his back to the fire, and buried his bleeding face in his hands. And Hook Nose started playing again, while the Carcajou inspected the cook's wound. Through it all Jack's father continued to stare at the ground.

But now Bonesteel signaled Jack to prepare to do what they had come to do. Cautiously Jack moved back behind a tree and gave the owl cry.

The Carcajou looked up—then down again. Hook Nose paused in the middle of a phrase—and went on playing. But Jack's father lifted his eyes cautiously and looked around.

Jack signaled to Bonesteel and Joshua that they should all move back deeper into the swamp. "He will come," he said, and gave the cry again.

Presently an owl answered faintly off to the left. They moved farther away. All they heard was the sustained high note of the myriad mosquitoes swarming around their heads. Jack gave the cry again.

Near at hand something caused a ripple on the surface of a fetid pool, something like a small creature sliding beneath the scum. Jack called softly. A shadow detached itself and came toward them. Jack and his father stood face to face. The Pilot clasped Jack in his arms.

"Jack, Jack, my boy, what are you a-doing here? Don't you know you're in a power of danger?"

"I'm safe, Papa, but not you."

Bonesteel knew he and Joshua had no right to watch. Even so, he did. He made his voice harsh.

"You are the one who is in danger, Pilot. And we have risked our honor and perhaps our lives to come and tell you. But I doubt if you would know what loyalty to one's country means."

"Yes, yes," the Pilot mumbled.

"So you must come back with us immediately. Leave everything and come now."

A stubbornness came into the Pilot's face. He shook his head.

"Papa, if they catch the gang you will be hanged. It is because Potts is a spy, though we have not told."

"But the General will find out soon enough," Bonesteel added angrily. "Then we'll all be in trouble."

The Pilot slid his eyes down to the ground. He moved his head from side to side. His lips formed soundless words.

Impatient as Bonesteel was, he could see that the Pilot was engaged in some sort of titanic struggle with himself. The way he stood with his legs apart; the way he held his arms stiff straight down; the way he clenched and unclenched his hands; the way he heaved his chest. The Pilot looked up appealingly, then spoke his decision. "Even for that it is impossible, Jackie, boy. Sometime I come, yes. At present, no. I do not run away from myself like that."

Bonesteel frowned, not understanding. Jack turned away.

Urgently the Pilot stepped toward Jack. "I have not left you, Jack. I have not. But something I must do first. You understand, don't you?" He put a trembling hand on Jack's shoulder. Jack did not move. The Pilot groaned and let his hand drop. He turned to Bonesteel.

"I asked you once, sir, I ask you again: take care of my Jack. You are the one good man I know. I don't want the Carcajou to get him. My Jack, he's a fine boy. . . . My Jack is the best boy in the whole world."

After that appeal Bonesteel knew he could not help himself. No matter what he had risked he could do nothing else but put his heart into his reply. "You know I will, Pilot. I give you my word. I will take care of Jack."

"Thank you, sir. Someday I come back a different man. Then I make it all up to you. Then you know all."

Suddenly there were rushing sounds all around. Bonesteel raised his gun. It was snatched from him. A voice snarled, "For you, schoolmaster!" He half turned. Hook Nose was aiming a blow at his head. There was a blinding light. Bonesteel felt himself falling, floating to the ground. He was vaguely aware of feet scuffling around him, stepping on him, kicking him. But he didn't mind. He was so very comfortable. He thought he heard someone call, "Here, Mr. Standish. Over here!" And there were distant sounds of cries and blows. Then he was floating again, rapidly, roughly—and was finally dumped carelessly on the ground.

Bonesteel licked his dry lips and slowly opened his eyes. He wanted to tell Jack and Joshua he was all right, that everything was fine. He did try to say it, but then near his face appeared a bloody bandage on a thigh. Bonesteel looked up into a lean, sallow face. The face broke into an uneven smile, and said, "Pardon, Mister Teach. I am Laroque."

Weakly, Bonesteel felt for his gun.

"The gun is not here. The Carcajou take it from you. You don't remember?"

Bonesteel licked his lips again. "Laroque, you devil." He saw that the only effect of calling him that was another twisted smile and a twinkle from the man's earring.

"Quite possibly the devil is a relation of mine." Laroque laughed. "But do not distress yourself. For I must speak quick. Then I must go."

Bonesteel felt his jaw drop open.

"It is I, Laroque, who save you when Jack cry out, 'Here. Mr. Standish. Over here!' You think Mr. Standish mind me be him?"

Bonesteel searched for words, but couldn't find any.

"That good trick. But you don't remember. No?"

Now Laroque was standing up and motioning to Jack, and Jack was leaning down. Laroque was squatting again.

"Listen, Mister Teach. Jack must not fear for his father. I, Laroque, am his friend." Laroque laughed softly. "Though you do not believe that, yet it is so." Then he said, "To you, Mister Teach, I say Laroque once not what you see now."

Suddenly Bonesteel was telling himself that here again he must revise his opinion about a man. There were so many questions. He struggled to sit up. Gently, Laroque hastened to help him.

Laroque was speaking to him again. "But if I remind you, Mister Teach, that there is a little good, sometimes, in a very bad man—believe me, I am tell you very much truth. And I, too, want you very much to keep Jack." Dramatically, Laroque leaped up. "Laroque is still the man of principle!"

And Bonesteel felt himself trying desperately to believe the urgent, almost pathetic, expression on Laroque's face.

In the next instant this astonishing villain was bowing in a courtly manner, and turning, and vanishing into the darkness.

Bonesteel put his head in his hands. All this, and the

86

splitting headache he had, were too much. And when there was so much to get straight!

After a time Joshua came to him. "When you want to go I've got the *South Wind* handy."

Bonesteel looked up. Joshua was grinning grandly— but behind him Jack was standing with his back toward them.

When Bonesteel spoke to answer Joshua, he saw that Jack moved away and sat down alone.

10

THEY WERE all there in storekeeper Benson's respectable upstairs parlor: Bonesteel and Jack; the Bensons, including Joshua's aunt; and Matthew Standish, who had just returned from Canada. It had taken all of Bonesteel's persuasive ability even to get Mr. Benson to listen. And now, Bonesteel said to himself, it was just one more thing that had to happen because he had befriended Jack. . . . Why didn't people understand?

Mr. Benson was jerking his eyes back and forth over Bonesteel's person. Bonesteel was not even trying to listen. He was watching Mr. Benson's eyes. Mr. Benson was obviously picking out the things about Bonesteel that he didn't like. "And he seems to be dwelling with particular pleasure on that bruise on my temple where Hook Nose hit me," Bonesteel thought ruefully.

"And what is more"—Mr. Benson was pounding the table—"I don't like your ideas about people, either, or your crazy ideals. . . . And I think it's too bad that rap you got on your head wasn't a lot harder."

"I'm terribly sorry about all this, sir. I—"

"Bosh! If you had to risk your life like that, why

did you have to take my son along with this—with this"
—he jabbed his finger at Jack—"young savage here. You
remember what Mr. Wall said, don't you?"

Bonesteel watched Mr. Benson press his knuckles on
the table top, and drop his head. He could see that he
was completely exhausted. Bonesteel felt sorry for him
—and yet again, he didn't.

Mr. Benson raised his haggard face. "Don't I have any
rights to my son?"

Bonesteel didn't answer.

Mr. Benson shook his head in disbelief. "You have
to take him up to Goose Pond Swamp and try to rescue
a man who everybody says is a worthless drunk—rescue
him from the most vicious gang this lake has ever seen.
Rescue! By his own words he didn't want to be rescued."

Jack made a quick movement. Bonesteel slipped his
arm through Jack's.

Matthew Standish cleared his throat noisily. "I reckon
it's time I stuck my nose into this, friend Benson."

Mr. Benson's voice was weary. "You too?"

"Yes, me too. I'll be a sort of counsel for the defense.
I'll take Hosea first—Mister Teach, Jack calls him, and
for good reason, as you'll see."

Bonesteel had a quick flash of memory. The General
had said something like that back there on the *Vermont*.
What would the General or Matthew call him now if
they knew the whole story? His heart sank.

"Now I think I know what's going on in Mister Teach's
head. He'd go through the torments of the damned for
Jack here, or for any other worthy boy."

89

Mr. Benson started to say something. Mr. Standish held up his hand.

"Hosea is Hosea. And his kind will do anything for a boy they believe in. Maybe you'll argue he's younger than you or I, and so maybe he's not supposed to have so much sense as we have. Maybe yes, maybe no. But he knows how valuable boys are. And he's got the courage of his convictions. His kind is rare. Believe you'll allow that?"

Bonesteel felt himself taking hold again. It was good to hear himself summed up like that by a man he trusted.

"Now, Jack here," Matthew went on, "and I'd be right proud to have a boy like Jack—Jack did just right. I admire him. Fact is, he did so right it makes the whole thing kinda noble. Now doesn't it?"

"Well, some folks say—"

Mr. Standish held up his hand. "I believe the Good Book has something to say, too. If I was a father like you I'd be proud to let my boy be with Hosea."

Joshua's father searched Matthew's face. Matthew nodded, and said, "It's time to forget and forgive all around. What with the invasion coming, we might be sorry someday we spent our time chewing on each other." He blinked soberly. "Like you've been doing here today."

Mr. Benson wanted to say something but his sister shook her head. "Not now, brother. Everybody understands."

"All right," he replied. Avoiding Bonesteel's eyes, he staggered to a chair in the corner.

Bonesteel cleared his throat to speak, but a voice inside

him said no. This had all turned out better than he had hoped. Jack had had a chance to see how good folks settle their differences. It must be quite a contrast to the swamp. And it looked as though even Mr. Benson might one day be Jack's friend.

Bonesteel had done all he could; and had taken all he could, for that matter, and now he wanted to get away. He had to face up to himself about Potts being a spy. But when he started to leave, Mr. Benson laid his arm across Jack's shoulder.

"We want you to stay for dinner, Jack. And you too, Hosea. And Matthew."

Angrily Jack backed away. But Bonesteel saw the others nodding their heads. He and Jack couldn't go yet. He said, "It's nice of Mr. Benson to ask us, Jack. We should stay."

Jack gave a sullen answer. "Me, I stay. But I don't want to."

Joshua's aunt's smile was determined. "We are glad you and Joshua are such good friends, Jack.... My goodness, you two boys must be hungry. Now while you are cleaning up from the swamp I'll hustle dinner. I won't take long."

Matthew said, "And I just got back from Canada. Quite a trip. Guess I could do with a little soap and water myself."

Joshua lead them out on to the backstairs porch where, in summer, Aunt Charity kept the washstand.

While they were cleaning up, Bonesteel heard Joshua's father and aunt talking and moving about in the kitchen. He said, "I think you've made two good friends, in there,

Jack. Friendship and forgiveness, they go together, you know."

Matthew stopped lathering his hands. "And don't forget, boy, I'm number three."

Jack did not reply, and from the look on his Indian face, Bonesteel had a fear for the first time since the closing of school that he might do something desperate.

When they went back into the kitchen Bonesteel saw that the table had been pulled out from the wall and was covered with a fine checkered tablecloth and good-smelling food in heavy cream-white dishes with gilt edges. He saw Joshua smile. Bonesteel suspected that Joshua's aunt had done these things for Jack, and that Joshua knew it.

After Matthew asked the blessing, and they sat down, Joshua's aunt tried to start a conversation, but it didn't go very well. Finally, Mr. Benson made a great effort. He laid down his knife and fork, and cleared his throat. "Matthew, how are things in Canada?"

Matthew looked up soberly. "Bad—very bad."

"They coming down this way?"

"Either here or down through Vermont. I'd say here."

"Can they do it?"

The last thing Bonesteel wanted to hear about was the invasion, but Matthew swung into it. "I'll tell you some things about the British, and you can judge for yourself. Some other things I won't tell, of course. I'm going to report them to the General. You understand why I can't tell everything."

Bonesteel found himself listening now in spite of himself.

"Tell what you can," Mr. Benson said. "I haven't been paying as much attention to this war as I should."

"All right. I'll start by saying the British have got themselves a real army at St. Johns. They've got lots of regulars there, and more coming all the time."

"From England?"

"From England. Not very big men, but lean and cordy, and sassy. Some of 'em have little elephants on their buttons—Wellington's India veterans fresh from the continent of Europe."

Bonesteel looked quickly at the boys.

"The newspapers said they might come," Mr. Benson said.

"They have. And since that's no secret I'll add they've got Swiss mercenaries, a whole regiment. Muscular fellows, and quick-tempered."

"Canadians?" Bonesteel asked.

"Naturally, Hosea. Lots of them. Descendants of Loyalists who got out of this country during the Revolution."

"It's only natural they'd want to fight," Bonesteel heard himself say.

"They've got light dragoons, rocketeers, sappers—and a lot more kinds of specialists. All of them have had battle experience."

Bonesteel looked at his plate. He did not want to hear the answer to his next question, but he had to know. "How are they supplied?"

Jack and Joshua looked quickly at him.

"The best—the very best." Matthew said.

"Flour?"

"Flour. All they want."

Mr. Benson said, "I haven't seen any white flour for a year."

Bonesteel was getting closer. "Rum?"

"Oh yes, rum. They always go strong on rum. Regular issue."

"Beef?" Bonesteel licked his lips. "Do they seem to get beef?"

"Beef, Hosea? I'll say they get beef. They've been buying beef all over Canada"—Matthew cleared his throat—"and elsewhere for a long time."

Bonesteel pressed his lips tightly together. Clearly he heard Mr. Benson say, "I was talking to our Collector of Customs yesterday. Said he just wrote a letter to the War Department in Washington about the traffic north in beef. Right through the lines, he said it goes. Said it is endangering our security."

And he heard Matthew reply, "Yes, I know. The General would like to stop that traffic. I'm working on that myself, in a way, among other things."

Bonesteel feared the next word, whatever it might be. But when Mr. Benson spoke, what he had to say was a complete surprise. "Joshua, this war—I wanted to save you from it. I won't any longer. T'wouldn't be right. It's bigger than you or me.... Matthew is going to ask Hosea to sail him to Canada soon. You can go along in the *South Wind*. I suppose Jack will go.... I have a hankering to make everything right."

Bonesteel saw everybody suddenly smiling at Jack.

94

Mr. Benson seemed to wait for some sort of reply. Jack said nothing. Mr. Benson reddened. "Er—this won't be any pleasure trip, Joshua, though Matthew won't expect Hosea to go beyond Macdonough's fleet at King's Bay."

Matthew said, "I'll go on from there alone."

Joshua's aunt hastened to say, "Until you go we would like Jack to stay here with Joshua, if he will?"

Joshua grinned. "He'll stay. Won't you, Jack?"

All Jack said was, "Thank you."

He didn't smile.

When the dinner was over Matthew Standish thanked the Bensons. "It was mighty nice of you folks to invite me. And I'm glad everything has turned out the way it has. It's the Lord's way. And now, if you'll excuse me, ma'am—friend Benson—I'm seeing the General this afternoon."

Bonesteel said, "Matthew, I want to go along with you."

"Well now, Hosea, my conversation with the General will be private."

"I didn't mean it that way. But there's something I've got to tell him."

"Hum. . . . Well, you'd better come along, then."

"And I want you to hear it too. After that I'll leave."

"Well, if it's that way, do come along."

Jack touched Bonesteel's arm. But Bonesteel wasn't in a frame of mind to think of two things at once. He shook his head. "You'd better stay here, Jack."

11

SIT DOWN, gentlemen. Good to see you again, Mister Teach."

Then the General saw Bonesteel's inflamed temple. "Not another fight with that stranger? . . . That was some battle while it lasted, eh, Standish?"

Bonesteel remained standing. He braced his legs apart and took a deep breath. "Yes, General, another fight with that same stranger."

The General leaped up. "You have? Where?"

Bonesteel glanced quickly at Matthew. "I'll come to that, sir. It's all part of something I should have reported some time ago. Now I'm here to tell you about it. . . . And you can judge me as you see fit."

Matthew leaned forward. "What are you talking about, Hosea?"

"You'll know soon enough, Matthew."

The General sat down. He studied Bonesteel's face. "Go ahead," he said.

"You are acquainted with a Plattsburg man by the name of Lycurgus Potts?"

"I won't say I'm acquainted, but I know who he is."

"Pardon me, General, but how has this man come to your attention?"

"Why, he started selling us beef some time ago—not very much, but some. We're desperate for supplies, you know. We placed an order with him just this week."

"So that's how he works it."

"Works what?"

"Did you know that he is also selling beef to the British?"

"Well, no. Of course not."

"And that he is also selling them information about our defenses here? Somehow when he is taking an order here he gets around—finds out things."

"That's not possible."

"He does, though. Or thinks he does. The British think he does."

Matthew interrupted. "Potts is just the kind of a weasel who could do it, General, and he has been showing considerable prosperity lately, if that's any indication."

Bonesteel turned to Standish. "It's all true, Matthew." He faced the General again. "And his contact with the British is that same British officer who travels with the *Black Sloop* Gang, and who, by the way, is the stranger I fought in the schoolyard."

Standish let out a long whistle, and the General demanded, "How do you know all this? And how long have you known it?"

"Some of it I've known for a long time. Part of it I suspected. Last night I got proof of everything."

Bonesteel told the whole story, from the night when

97

he saw Potts talking to Hook Nose on board the British sloop-of-war, through his own deal with Potts, through the incident at the swamp. He told about Jack and his father, and that that was the reason he had not reported before. He told about Laroque. He omitted nothing.

When he was done, the General went to the window. "You weren't thinking very straight, were you?"

"The only straight thinking I've done is to hope that the gang might have disposed of Potts by now, considering the way things happened at the swamp. Otherwise I was thinking of Jack. I got into this business so fast —but I can't say I didn't see where it was taking me."

"Isn't that the way a good man is caught sometimes? You can't think with your heart in time of war."

"I know that now."

"You can never do the right thing the wrong way." The General looked silently out the window. "Would you have any knowledge of how much damage has been done already?"

"I hope none. But I don't know."

The General turned around. "Do you recall when you brought that warning to the *Vermont* that I said a lot of folks around here will be shot at by the British before snow flies this winter?"

"Yes sir."

"Hadn't it occurred to you that more of them might be killed because you withheld this information?"

"No sir, it hadn't. I didn't think that far."

"Does it now?"

"Yes."

The General paused again, then, "Standish, you have just returned from Canada. Do you bring back knowledge of the size of the British army?"

"They've got 10,000 now, and they're expecting 4000 more."

Bonesteel felt the General's stern gaze, so different from his friendly smile. "Does that mean anything to you?... Can you add anything, Standish?"

"I think I can confirm Hosea's story."

"Well, well, go ahead."

"I found out there's somebody here who is selling military information to the British. He gets it quick—when he wants it. Passes it to somebody else, and that somebody else moves it fast."

"Has this been going on long?"

"Since spring. It fits Hosea's timing. Fact is, this is what I came to report about."

Again the General's stern gaze. "See, schoolmaster?"

Matthew continued. "Whoever gets this information here knows what to look for, or is told what to look for, and is in a position to get it."

"Such as—?"

"How many beeves are on order for the whole area for next month. How much powder we've stored, and where. Placement of bomb batteries and strength of same."

Bonesteel groaned, sat down, and put his head in his hands.

Matthew went on. "Strength of our blockhouses and forts. What plans we have to strengthen our defenses.

Location and names of our regiments and their strength —militia—like that."

The General exclaimed, "Great Caesar's ghost! Do they know all that?"

"If not, that's what they expect to find out."

"How did you find out all this?"

"Well, I preach the word of God around in Canada a little, General. Doing the Lord's work when I can. Also do a little smithing here and there. The British seem to think I'm harmless."

"Hum-m."

"But until now I couldn't find out who this spy is."

The General expelled a long breath. "Well, we know now, don't we? It's this man Potts. And we know how he does it."

"Yes sir. I guess we do. It's quite a setup, General." And Bonesteel felt Matthew's comforting hand.

Bonesteel looked up. "And the fellow who thinks with his heart instead of with his head, because he wants to save one Indian boy, is the one who let all this get started. And that's me."

"Yes, that's you," the General said.

Bonesteel squirmed under the General's penetrating stare.

The General started pacing back and forth. "Standish, will you vouch for Bonesteel here?"

"I'll vouch for him, General, all the way."

The General shoved his hands into his pockets and started talking in a way Bonesteel couldn't understand, impatient as he was to know what the General was going to do with him. The General said that he was a commanding officer in charge of a military area during a war, but that he was also a humane man with simple tastes. And then he went on telling how he'd like to resign his commission when the war was over and buy a farm and settle down in this wonderful North Country among these wonderful people.

Finally Bonesteel couldn't stand it any longer. He burst out, "What about me, sir? I'm ready to take my punishment."

"I was thinking about you when I said all that. All right, here it is." Bonesteel braced himself. "Now that I know about this gang, and this British officer, and this man Potts, I'm going to leave them right where they are. And I'm going to leave you right where you are, too."

"What?"

"Because you and I are going to feed Potts just the kind of information I want the enemy to get. I'll have those British running around in circles."

Bonesteel looked in amazement at Matthew.

The General went on. "And your part will be to get in with Potts and assure him that in spite of what happened at the swamp it's all right with you. That to protect Jack's father you'll say nothing about his being a spy. That you will play right along with him indefinitely, if necessary."

"I'll do it if it is at all possible," Bonesteel said, still slightly dizzy.

"Make it possible," the General ordered. "But I

wouldn't advise you to let yourself fall into the hands of those two vultures, the Carcajou and Hook Nose."

"Well—I'm taking Matthew Standish north in the *South Wind* as soon as he is ready to go back to Canada. Maybe I can make a contact then."

"Very well. Are you taking Jack and Joshua with you?"

"I had planned to. But there may be danger now."

"They are in this as deep as you are. Take them. I don't want them around here, knowing what they know."

"But General—"

"They will be no different from soldiers preparing for battle, or in one. Nor will you. I say, take them."

"Yes sir."

"Because if it gets out that Potts is a spy, and he hears about it and gets away, I will hold you personally responsible. . . . If the man is still alive, of course."

Bonesteel swallowed. "I understand that."

"So this had better work. But if you prefer, you can think of the opportunity you have of making up for what you have allowed to happen, and the chance of rendering your country a great service. . . . And Mister Teach—?"

Bonesteel noticed the change in the General's voice. "What is it, sir?"

"When this turns out as we hope it will, I think you will have achieved your purpose of giving Jack the example of a good and useful man. . . . That's what I was thinking of back there when I talked about settling down here one day. I envy you your point of view.

Maybe I am just a little envious of you, personally. I think you're a good man." The General cleared his throat. "You are free to go now."

Bonesteel hurried his steps toward the bridge over the Saranac. At least, he must tell Jack his father was safe.

But when he got to the Bensons' they told him Jack had gone.

Greatly disturbed, Bonesteel hurried to his room. There he found a note propped up on his desk:

Your ways are not my ways. Your friends are not my friends. If my father die, I hate you. I go back to Black Sloop. Mr. Benson say my father no good. Me no good either. Goodbye, Teach.

Jack

Bonesteel's heart was heavy. He had regained his self-respect, but he had lost Jack. Couldn't he have both, especially in a frontier town? Or were all the Mr. Walls in the world right, after all?

12

UNTIL STANDISH was ready to go, Bonesteel determined to haunt the cedars back of Potts's house in the bare outside chance Potts might come home. But after a night and a day of this the General told Bonesteel that Potts was probably staying on the *Black Sloop*.

"I'm sending Standish to Commodore Macdonough tomorrow with a rather doleful message. He'll go on to Canada from there. Here's your chance to see the fleet and start looking for Potts."

"I'm eager to get at it," Bonesteel said.

Bonesteel knew the General was studying him. "Mister Teach, I'm going to tell you Standish's message. It will give new importance to your task.... The city of Washington has been raided and burned by the British."

Bonesteel was aghast. "Why, that can't be! That's the capital of the country!"

"It happened all right. And although the British retreated immediately, the effect upon the minds of our people—well—" The General's voice trailed off, and picked up again. "Anyway, we've got to use every trick now. You've got to contact Potts. You've got to be careful. It may take time."

Bonesteel could see that the General was worried.

As the *South Wind* overhauled the southern tip of Isle la Motte they strained their eyes to catch the first glimpse of the American fleet anchored at King's Bay. That's where the Commodore would be.

Joshua sang out first. "I see something!"

Matthew Standish squinted into the distance. "In this sun? Boy, your eyes are good."

Bonesteel shaded his eyes. "He's right. There's movement there."

"They're making and taking in sail," Joshua announced.

"Probably exercising the galleys," Matthew said.

Joshua pointed. "There's the fleet! Over there to the west. There's the *Saratoga!* And there's the *Preble* and the *Ticonderoga!*"

Bonesteel nudged Joshua. "Isn't that the *Vermont* tied up to the *Saratoga?*"

Presently they were among the row-galleys. Crisp order came from the nearest. Her sail billowed down, her oars ran out. She foamed toward the *South Wind*. Her bow gun seemed to grow larger and more ominous At the last minute she hoisted sail and veered away.

"Pretty—pretty." Matthews eyes shone.

Bonesteel said, "Maybe Amos would have some information about the *Black Sloop*."

All was activity when they stepped aboard the *Saratoga*. As they saluted the flag a young lieutenant stepped briskly toward them. Matthew introduced himself and said they had business with the Commodore.

The lieutenant strode toward the quarterdeck. Presently he returned. "Captain Macdonough will see you. This way, please."

As they walked aft along the long clean deck Bonesteel noted gun crew after gun crew smartly practicing at the guns. He recognized farm hands, rough lake hands, seamen—all welded into a single purpose. He wondered if Hook Nose had any way of finding out about this.

His eyes wandered up the tall masts towering aloft. They dropped back down the shrouds and lifted up again to the intricate pattern of rigging—and finally to the fighting tops. He felt guilty giving his time and thought to anything that did not concern the *Black Sloop* or Potts, but Bonesteel had to admit to himself that if the invasion came he wanted to be aboard this ship.

At the quarterdeck the tall, sandy-haired Macdonough was extending his hand. "I'm glad to know you, Mr. Bonesteel."

Bonesteel looked at the blue uniform and epaulets at the shoulders. "I'm glad to know you, sir."

"I see you were looking our ship over. Wouldn't believe her timbers were trees standing in the forest only forty days before she was launched, would you? She'll take the British *Confiance*."

"That she will," Bonesteel replied vigorously.

And then Matthew was telling the Commodore about Washington.

"I shall tell the men. It's all they need to know." The Commodore turned to Bonesteel and Joshua. "I want you to stay and hear this."

It stirred Bonesteel to see the tough young officers of the American Navy come aboard. Each in his own way was alert as with firm steps and puzzled faces they hurried aft. He noticed that the gun crews were intensely curious, and that they watched covertly as the officers hurried by.

He looked overside. Clustered around the ship were the galleys. Their crews were staring up at the quarterdeck.

And then suddenly all was quiet. Bonesteel could hear no human sound throughout the fleet.

Commodore Macdonough told about Washington. His crisp words lashed the officers to anger. When he finished he pulled out his handkerchief and mopped his brow. He was well nigh trembling with anger himself. He told the officers to go back and tell the men.

Bonesteel watched the officers run back down the long deck.

Soon an angry growl grew throughout the fleet, grew and died down, grew again and burst into a defiant yell that sent the sea gulls wheeling off in frightened flight.

Macdonough seized his megaphone and swung himself up into the shrouds. The yelling stopped. He shouted, "We all know how we feel now! I guess we all know what to do now!"

Bonesteel was breathing hard too. Suddenly Macdonough's words had a personal meaning for him. The General had told him not to let the Carcajou catch him. He would avoid that, of course. But even getting caught wouldn't matter if that was the only way he could make the General's plan work.

13

AFTER THEY PUT Standish ashore they
hastened to the *Vermont*. The good
Captain threw out his arms happily to greet them.

Familiar sounds of metal striking metal came to them
from the engine hatch. Bonesteel took this to mean that
it was the same old engine with the same old trouble.

"Is Amos down there, Captain?" Bonesteel asked.

The Captain nodded his head, and bellowed, "Amos!"

Amos's head appeared above the hatch coaming. He
blinked in the sunlight and then spied his friends.
"Eeyow! What are you all doing on my steamboat?"
He leaped out on deck.

Joshua grinned. But Amos's responding grin suddenly drained away. His mahogany face turned an un-
natural color.

Bonesteel had to laugh. "What's the matter, Amos?"

"Is you all right, Mister Teach? Is you—please, sir?"

Bonesteel looked at himself. "You know I'm all right."

Amos persisted, more upset. "Hain't had no troubles?"

"No. No troubles."

"Oh lawdy. Then you is going to have."

The Captain interrupted to ask what this was all about. "You haven't been dreaming again, have you, Amos?" he said.

"Yes sir, Captain. I have."

"You have?"

Bonesteel saw the Captain's eyes were bulging.

"Well, for heaven's sake, what about this time?"

Amos stretched his arm toward Bonesteel. "About him. . . . Stay off the lake, Mister Teach. Stay off the lake! That's what I drumpt."

Bonesteel started to laugh again, but the Captain seized his arm. "Don't laugh. I used to laugh at his dreams. But I don't any more."

Amos groaned, "It was awful."

"What was?" Bonesteel demanded impatiently.

Amos rolled his eyes. "I can't rightly say, sir. But just stay off the lake. Please sir, for Amos Lash. There ain't so many of you now. Jack, he's gone. I drumpt that too."

Bonesteel saw Joshua stare, but he refused to accept it. "You probably heard about Jack somewhere, Amos. And I'm not frightened by dreams."

"My dreams comes true. I don't like them to, but they do."

Bonesteel snorted in disgust.

It wasn't a very pleasant visit after that, and when he went overside Bonesteel was not in a very good mood. Nor was he helped any by the Captain. When they were sailing away Bonesteel saw the Captain lean far out over the rail, cup one hand to his mouth, and point back.

He heard him faintly, "Watch out for that Amos's dreams, or maybe you'll be sorry."

Then, suddenly, Bonesteel remembered that he hadn't asked Amos if he knew anything about where the *Black Sloop* might be. He half turned the boat around to go back. But angrily he decided against it. If Amos had an answer it would only be superstitious hokus-pokus. Bonesteel refused to give in to that sort of thing. He straightened away south again.

Bonesteel could see, or thought he could see, that Joshua was worrying about Amos's dream. So now, wouldn't it be better to get Joshua back to Plattsburg safe in his home first, General or no General?

If it were Jack sitting there it would be different. Jack had grown up fast and rough and free, becoming a man before his time. He could take care of himself.

But Joshua had been given his freedom only a week ago, and then only because Matthew Standish had made Mr. Benson open his hand, in a manner of speaking, and let Joshua go. . . . Yet, before that, at the swamp, Joshua had shown the decision and loyalty of a man. But—just the same—it was probably better to take him back first.

Bonesteel knew himself well enough to know he was not cut out of the same pattern as the General. The General was a man of cold action who had said to take the boys along because it was the same as being in a battle. But it was different now. Jack was gone. And Bonesteel had already decided to forget about his own safety. He asked himself if Amos's dreams about Jack and the lake had after all upset him. He shook himself free from such thinking. No, it was just that he was a man of heart.

Bonesteel saw that Joshua was watching him, blue eyes steady, face unsmiling. He said, "I hope you're not thinking about Amos?"

"Not exactly," Joshua replied.

Bonesteel tipped his head to one side and smiled.

"Well, I was thinking about Amos some," Joshua said, "but mostly I guess I was thinking about how my father has been planning my life so I will take over the store someday. But now—"

"You shouldn't disappoint him there. It's a good opportunity."

"He thinks a merchant ought to be a good influence in a town, especially a frontier town like Plattsburg. I think so too."

Here was a Joshua Bonesteel hadn't seen before.

"But it took Matthew Standish to make him see that I couldn't become that kind of a man until I had taken part in the times I live in."

"I don't think your father thinks you are lost to him now."

"Oh, I'm not going to disappoint him."

Bonesteel realized that heretofore he had thought of Joshua only as Jack's friend. Now he was seeing him as a separate person. "I see." He smiled warmly. "I see a great deal."

And he was all the more glad he had decided to get Joshua back to town. He wouldn't be the one to risk such a fine boy. Let somebody else do that.

It was one of those bright out-of-doors afternoons.
The lake was running free and clear, and the mid-August
sunlight was doing wonderful things to the water. Bonesteel stood up, looked all around, and squared his shoulders. The strong wind from the south flattened his shirt
against his muscular chest and tossed his dark hair about.

"That's a great sailing wind. We'll be home sometime
tonight."

Joshua was surprised. "Home? I thought we were
going to look for the *Black Sloop*."

"I think I'll start at Valcour."

"Why not up here?"

Bonesteel side-stepped. "Oh, they wouldn't be out on
the lake on a bright day like this."

Joshua wanted to argue about it, but Bonesteel
wouldn't. "Let's talk about something else. What you
said about your father and the store—"

"Sure, but—"

"Now take this North Country. It can be something
different in this wicked world. You're worth saving for
it " Bonesteel had the smile of a man thinking beautiful
thoughts.

Joshua laughed. "Me? Saving? I don't understand."

"Yep. It's more than just scenery. It's great and good.
. . . Different."

Joshua nodded his head puzzled. "Well, sure. I've
thought about that."

"Fine—fine!" Bonesteel realized he wasn't making
much sense to Joshua, but for some reason he didn't
care.

The *South Wind* was now on the starboard reach, and Bonesteel was giving his attention to the approaching shoreline of North Hero Island. He put the tiller over and dodged the boom.

"So I'll put the question to you, Joshua," he said. "In the light of what I have just been saying, is there any place on this lake for the Carcajou or for Amos's dreams?" Bonesteel laughed into the wind.

Their westing had brought them well over toward Long Point, on the other side of which lay the great bay which Bonesteel and Jack had watched the night of the affair in the swamp.

Suddenly Joshua leaped up. "Look! Look there!"

Lunging toward them through the tricky passage in Long Point Reef was the *Black Sloop*.

"No!" Bonesteel shouted. "Not yet! I've got to get you back to town first."

He jammed the tiller over. The *South Wind* fled southeastward.

One beat to windward and Jack knew his father, the Pilot, would put the *Black Sloop* through the passage. When they were in it he would tell Jack to jump overboard and swim along the reef to shore. The *Black Sloop* couldn't follow him. Once in the passage it would have to go through. By that time Jack would be safe.

Waiting for his time, Jack set himself to watch all that would be happening when the Carcajou discovered something was wrong. He must not jump too soon or too late.

He saw the Carcajou limp angrily aft. "Where do you think you're a-going, Pilot?"

"Through here. Save time."

"Ye dum' fool, that there's the meanest passage on the Lake. Ye'll pile her up!"

"Always wanted to try it. Better you go forward and watch for rocks." Confidently the Pilot turned his back on the Carcajou and looked toward the New York shore to line up his bearings.

The Carcajou scampered forward. "If ye bust us open I'll cave your fool head in."

Now Jack's father was whispering pleadingly to him. Jack saw his eyes soft and kind. "Better you get ready to jump when I tells you to." Jack believed he must have frowned because his father said, "Please, Jack. You swim back to the point. Me, I'll shave them rocks so close it'll make that Carcajou crazy and he won't have no time to see what you're a-doing. You've just got to go back to Mister Teach."

At that moment Jack saw there was some commotion up forward. The Carcajou had forgotten the channel and was pointing out on the lake and was jumping up and down and shaking as though he had the ague.

He leaped again and let out a roar. "There he be! Now I've got him! Cook, you fetch me that Mister Teach's gun." He turned and shouted back, "Pilot, you scrape us now and I'll kill ye!"

"What is it?" Jack asked his father.

The cook brought the gun. The Carcajou crooked his free arm around it. As though to answer Jack's question he shouted, "Now I'm catching me that there meddling schoolmaster!"

"Now you jump," Jack's father whispered hoarsely.

"No, no! I don't go now!"

The Carcajou yelled, "Hook Nose, go ye aft and keep an eye on that Pilot."

Laroque reached for his stiletto. "Drop it, Frenchy," the Carcajou barked. Laroque obeyed.

The Carcajou tossed a pistol to the cook. "Here, you krauthead, watch Laroque."

The Carcajou was laughing hard. "Come here, Potts. I'll show ye how it's done."

Jack saw the fat little spy rush to the rail and kneel beside the Carcajou, peer ahead, and squeal hysterically.

It was Jack, this time, who buried his face in his hands and groaned.

Bonesteel believed in himself and in his boat. And out here off Long Point, halfway between the American fleet and Plattsburg, in broad daylight—to be taken by the Carcajou? It struck him funny.

He looked at Joshua's long face and laughed harder. "Come on, boy, you're about to see some real sailing. Break out a smile there."

Joshua smiled weakly.

"And here we go," Bonesteel shouted. "Hang on!"

The *South Wind* answered to his hand. She heeled sharply and thundered forward. Joshua climbed to the weather rail and lay along the deck.

The *Black Sloop* heeled also, her live body lunging at the waves.

It was tack against tack; skill against skill; hunter and prey.

The *Black Sloop* was gaining.

On the *South Wind* they could see the Carcajou steady himself against the rail. Now he was raising the gun, the distance was that short.

Twice the Carcajou raised the gun. Twice Bonesteel saw him chew angrily. But the noise of wind and spray deafened him so that he could not hear.

Bonesteel shouted, "He'll be lucky if he even hits Vermont State. I'll sail this old hooker to Plattsburg, and you'll see—"

The Carcajou fired.

Bonesteel wondered why that small puff of gunsmoke grew so big.

Joshua felt the *South Wind* come up into the wind and shudder there. Then he saw Mister Teach slump to the floor, and a white crease on the side of his head slowly turn red.

14

AT FIRST Bonesteel felt only a rocking motion. Then he opened his eyes. Everything was blurred. Someone was kneeling beside him. He strove to see who it was. It was Joshua, of course. He was content to close his eyes again.

But not for long. He must open his eyes once more. He looked up this time. Strange—there were feet, legs, men, all around him. He made an effort to focus his sight.

Suddenly, they were all there: Hook Nose, and behind him was Potts. Farther back was Laroque. Directly in front was the Carcajou.

He and Joshua were captives on the *Black Sloop*.

The Carcajou's bellowing laughter beat the air. "What have you got to say for yourself now, you Plattsburg pig of a schoolmaster?"

"He can't speak yet. He's wounded." That was Joshua.

"Oh yes he can. Like this."

Bonesteel saw the kick coming, but he was too weak to dodge.

"All the time I wait. And what I wait for falls in my

hand like a poor sick little bird. And who is it? I'll tell you. It's that there pig of a Mister Teach!" He stopped in front of Bonesteel and kicked him viciously again. "I'm the king of the lake! I win! I win! ... Well, *Mister* Teach, what have you got to say for yourself now?"

Dazed and hurt as he was, Bonesteel would take no more of that. With what consciousness he had left he would struggle to stand up. Delighted to see him try, the Carcajou waited until he was swaying on his feet. Then he grabbed him by the shirt.

"You heard me! Speak up!"

As Bonesteel made his last weak effort to resist, a fox-like face somehow got in the way. "One moment, Carcajou," the face said. "The Pilot wish you to come aft and tell Jack what to do with the *South Wind*."

"Tell him—" the Carcajou roared.

Laroque's voice sounded pleasantly smooth to Bonesteel. "Better you tell him yourself. Or maybe Jack take the *South Wind* back to Plattsburg?"

"I'll tell him!" The Carcajou charged aft. "He'll do none of that!"

While Potts and Hook Nose were hurrying aft too, Bonesteel heard the Carcajou yelling directions to Jack, who must have been in the *South Wind* astern of the *Black Sloop*.

Bonesteel slumped back to the deck. Laroque waited until they were surely alone. Then Bonesteel saw a twisted smile come upon Laroque's face. "Sometimes the Carcajou is very stupid. You wait here. I return in one instant."

Bonesteel closed his eyes and whispered, "Amos's dream. Poor Joshua—poor Joshua."

A hand touched his shoulder. He opened his eyes. Laroque was there holding Jack's dog. "Look. I have here one friend for you." Laroque released the dog. Little Loup pressed his small body against Bonesteel and whined affectionately.

Laroque said, "This I have to say to Mister Teach and Joshua. You are in great danger. But do not show grief. If you do, the Carcajou please to make you more grief."

Little Loup started sniffing Bonesteel's wound.

"The big German tie the dog in the lazarette. But— pht! I am the man of principle. No?"

Bonesteel hugged the dog. "You sure are."

"Good. Now three things I tell you—"

"Go ahead," Bonesteel said weakly. "Would appreciate any advice."

"One: Your one job now is to stay alive—to survive. Think only of that."

Bonesteel nodded.

"Two: So it is necessary for you both to be tough. Laroque have much experience in that. He know."

"Be tough," Bonesteel roused himself to say.

"Three: This is for Joshua. After the while you walk back to the Pilot. You look back on the lake. You see Jack with Mister Teach's boat. When it is darker you jump overboard. Swim to Jack. Get away."

"No!" Joshua said. "I won't leave Mister Teach."

Bonesteel was suddenly almost himself. "Yes you will, Joshua. You must get back to the General, and tell him that with Laroque's help I am about to succeed. . . . And it will be your chance to get Jack away from here. Do that, Joshua, do that. I beg you."

A confident grin spread over Joshua's face. "You just watch the storekeeper's boy. I'll get Jack away, and then we will take up where you leave off."

"Good boy," Bonesteel whispered and closed his eyes.

It must have been hours later—or was it? Bonesteel had lost all sense of time—that he heard a distant splash. There was running of feet, and somewhere aft much cursing and howling by the Carcajou. In restless half-consciousness Bonesteel waited. At last someone was whispering in his ear. It was Laroque.

"The boys got away, Mister Teach. They go back to Plattsburg. The Carcajou fit to be tied, but he can do nothing."

Bonesteel opened his eyes. It was dark. "That's good. Now tell Potts"—his voice got stronger—"tell Potts that I've got news for him that will save his filthy neck. Tell them all. Tell them the pig of a schoolmaster has saved their lives, even though they are all enemies of my country. And that goes for you too, Laroque. I am being tough."

Early the next morning Bonesteel was awakened by Laroque, who was whispering softly in his ear. "Mister Teach, you awake?"

"Yes, what is it?"

"Big argument go on for half the night."

"What about?"

"You. Potts want to hold you for ransom. The Carcajou want to kill you and throw you into the lake. And Hook Nose want to have you. Who you think win?"

"I'm sure I don't know."

"Hook Nose. He pay Carcajou plenty money for you."

"So now what happens?"

"That I do not know. But at least you stay alive."

15

FOR THREE DAYS Bonesteel lay there on that damp straw. He watched the moisture collect on the bluestone vault overhead, and drip—drip—to the floor and pass away down the smelly drain in the corner. Once each day a small shutter in the nail-studded oaken door squeaked open. Part of a sour face appeared, and then a small amount of vile food. Bonesteel had to get up quickly to take the food—or, said the surly voice that went with the face, "I'll throw it on the floor, and you can eat your victuals from there, if the rats don't get it first."

Once a British army surgeon came to dress his wound. Bonesteel asked the man where they were. But he got no more than a grunt for an answer. He felt very lonely. ... Hook Nose certainly had influence.

But Bonesteel had bits of memory to comfort him. He remembered quite clearly explaining to Potts and Hook Nose and the Carcajou that he had kept the secret of Potts's spying, and that Jack and Joshua would cut their tongues out before they would say anything. The gang had wanted to know why. He had replied with as much of a laugh as he could muster that it was for the Pilot's safety, not for theirs. And they'd better be good to the Pilot for that reason. Their lives depended upon him.

Then he remembered, but not so well, a long rough ride in a high two-wheeled cart. It must have been a French-Canadian kind of cart. And it seemed that Hook Nose had said earlier that not caring about protecting the gang personally, and wanting to save Bonesteel for his own revenge later, made it a lot easier to send him where he was now going.

So now, where had Hook Nose sent him? It was all-important to know. He even recalled vaguely a ride across a river—perhaps it was a river—in a rowboat. But that didn't help much.

"Come on, Yank, come on! Now up with ye!"

Bonesteel felt rough hands seize him and stand him on his feet.

"No more sleep, man. There's work to be done."

Still not awake, Bonesteel sagged back toward the straw. The hands caught him and shook him roughly, and from a point close to his nose the bull-like voice smote his ears. Bonesteel lifted heavy eyelids. A blue-eyed, grinning red face topped with a mass of sandy hair swayed not a foot from his nose, and in the center was the trumpet mouth from which was coming all the noise.

"Stand!" the trumpet bellowed. "I would see whereof you are made."

The hands which undoubtedly went with the face felt his shoulders and arms.

"Muscles. Aye, that's what I'm looking for." Steel-like fingers squeezed his biceps. "Well, well, there are

some, though ye wouldn't expect them on a Yankee."
The voice dropped to a rumble. "Now are ye awake?"

Bonesteel wondered if the man was becoming friendly.
He said, "Muscles I have when I'm well. But knowledge
of where I am I have not."

The trumpet became sarcastic. "And that's soon rem-
edied. Behind the British lines ye are, at Isle aux Noix
in the Richelieu River, right in the middle of it all, working for old Foghorn Macdonald, who has more work to
do than a thousand can do."

"Doing what?" Bonesteel asked, thinking that at least
the man liked to talk.

"So from Plattsburg, they send me one man with a
cracked head who mumbles in his sleep about a Muskrat
Jack and a Pilot. And of them I know nothing and care
less."

Bonesteel persisted. "Doing what, may I ask?"

"You are therefore all alone with no friends. And ye'd
better know that from the beginning. But you'll need
food for what ye are going to do. And we'll take care of
that straightway."

After Bonesteel had eaten heavily they rowed him to
the western shore of the river, where the vast preparations
the British were making for the invasion unrolled before
him. Stretching down the river he saw war galleys and
tops'l schooners with men, hundreds of men, crawling
over them. But dominating them all was a giant ship-
sloop, bigger than the *Saratoga*, being rigged and armed
by another crawling mass which was swarming over her

like bees over a comb of honey on a hot summer day just before a thunderstorm.

That ship must be the *Confiance*.

Everywhere there were hurrying Redcoats and their officers. Hurrying, demanding, mopping their brows, scurrying off, scurrying back, shaking papers, pointing at papers, pointing up and about, pointing everywhere.

It seemed to Bonesteel as though those who were not using their hands to work with were pointing at something or other.

"Hey, Plattsburg! Take this here adze to the master carpenter on yonder quarterdeck. Come on now, lively!" Bonesteel executed the order automatically. His mind was with the boys. He asked himself if they had got back to town all right. They must have.

"Give a hand here, man! Lay to that pile of lumber! Stack it over there!" It was the foghorn-voiced boss. He was well named. "No, over here! I've changed my mind. Jump!" Would Jack stay in Plattsburg now, with Joshua's folks perhaps?

"Jump!" "Step!" "Tote!" Would the General's plan work out all right now?

As the morning wore on Bonesteel's head began to spin. Things began to run together. The forest of masts, the stuck-pig squeal of pulley blocks, the thumping jar of guns lowered to decks, the smells of river water and tar and oxen and horses and men, the shouted orders. If he could only sit down somewhere.

But that was impossible. The boss's voice pushed him on.

So Bonesteel carried whip-sawn boards and coiled down rope and rolled round shot aboard the great raw newly launched *Confiance*.

The boss would take temporary interest in him. "What," he would ask, "do they call ye back where you come from?"

Bonesteel reeled to a stop and wiped the sweat from his eyes. "Teach. Mister Teach, I guess."

"Teach, eh? Well, Teach, we'll take that lake and land of yourn. You have nothing the like of all this. And ye'll be Mister Teach no more. Now get moving."

"Yes sir." Gripped by a nameless fear, Bonesteel staggered forward again. What if Hook Nose's plan should make him lose his identity and his purpose?

By midday the high, hot sun glared down upon the mad scene. This place was not like the broad lake with its spaces and winds. It was a close forest-embraced plain pierced by a marsh-bound river.

Bonesteel felt hemmed in. Fatigue had so drugged him that he hardly comprehended when an excited workman elbowed him and pointed to a column of scarlet soldiers on the nearby dusty road.

A mounted officer was raising his hand and was barking an order. The soldiers halted stiffly. The officer rode toward the boss and said something to him which caused both men to laugh uproariously. The boss turned to the workmen who were watching from the *Confiance*. He raised his hand, and shouted, "Here's one for ye, men. The city of Washington, that which they call the capital of the rebel nation to the south, has been took and burned by our King's troops. . . . Haw haw haw! . . . Pass that along!"

At the end of the long aching day Bonesteel threw himself down on the straw too tired to eat. As though from years ago Laroque's voice came to him: "Your one job now is to stay alive."

And so Bonesteel started arguing with himself. "I've got to fight, haven't I? So I've got to stay alive, haven't I? . . . Got to be tough. . . . Dear God, can I be tough enough?"

16

WHEN BONESTEEL first saw the *Confiance* her masts had just been stepped, and her shrouds set. Later he saw her rigging set, her yards sent up, her halyards and braces rove, and her canvas bent. After that it was more guns aboard, more shot, powder, victuals, stores, crew, officers, and a furnace set up for hot shot. Then the eager word was passed: "Tomorrow, wind or not, we'll take her out of the river, and give her her trial run."

Bonesteel saw this evil ship as a mortal threat to his lake, his valley, his country, and himself. But he could not pounce upon it and tear it apart with his puny hands. No man could accomplish such a fantastic act of insane passion. He got away from that kind of daydreaming in a hurry.

There were practical things to do now. First he must stay alive. Laroque's advice was good. Be tough. Next he must appear to cooperate in everything he was told to do. If he didn't they would surely ship him off to some stinking prison in Quebec, or even England, if Hook Nose's arm was long enough. Next he must gather all the information he could about the *Confiance,* so that if and when he escaped he could strike a telling blow by reporting it.   And finally, he must escape.

Until now Bonesteel had done all he could to save others: Jack, Joshua, Amos, even Lycurgus Potts.   But now his very being was at stake.   And he must save himself with honor.

The hardest and most dangerous animal to keep in a trap is man, Bonesteel thought.   So enough of thinking with the heart.   The time had come to think with the head.

On the first of September, three disheartening rumors fell upon him.   A British regiment had occupied an American town just over the border and was sweeping up teams and wagons.   Commodore Macdonough had moved his fleet south to Plattsburg Bay.   And, worst of all, 3000 American regulars had been marched away from Plattsburg—destination, of all places, the Niagara frontier.

The boss stood by and laughed.   Bonesteel tried to make it appear that it didn't matter too much to him.

Something else happened, worse than any of these.   On the morning after the rumor about the *Confiance,* Bonesteel went to the cook shack, where he was now eating, to get his usual breakfast of what he called horsemeat burgoo.   There he was roughly served by the cook's new helper.   The new helper was Amos Lash.

From a distance Amos began to abuse him.   "Eeyow! Look at that, now.   It's that Yankee prisoner I heard tell about."   Amos capered and pointed.   "I fix him!   This here Canada is the land of freedom."

Bonesteel said things, to which Amos replied, "Shut your mouth, white boy, or I'll fetch you a smack with this here skillet."

Bonesteel said under his breath, but so Amos could hear, "Some folks forget mighty quick."

Amos cuffed him soundly on the shoulder, and said, "I warned ye!" Then he said louder so everybody could hear, "Yes sir. I done forget I was a slave."

Bonesteel got up and left, followed by the coarse laughter of the crowd, with Amos's howling above all the rest.

The soft September haze that promised another North Country fall could not sweeten that day. The shock of seeing Amos that way, and the awful rumor about the American regulars, put Bonesteel away down again. And as if that were not enough, the sight of hundreds of British soldiers now passing south added the final weight. The brave memory of the American emplacements at Fort Izard and in Plattsburg on the south bank of the Saranac, and of Macdonough's fighting fleet—what was the use? What was the use of anything? . . . It was the rumbling and shouting and the tramp of marching feet that well nigh shook Bonesteel's world to pieces.

On the fourth of September the rumor spread that the British advance was encamped over halfway to Plattsburg. Poor General Macomb was doing all he could, but that was no more than a fleabite. Now the British were dividing at a fork in the road ten miles north of Plattsburg, and would take the town from two directions, while, on the lake, Commodore Macdonough was trying to make the most of a green fleet and an odd assortment of worn-out cannon. Somebody had called upon Vermont for volunteers but the governor had shaken his head in an emphatic no.

Bonesteel looked up from his work to see the genius of it all, the proud and haughty British commander, General Sir George Prevost, ride by, hand on hip, surrounded by his European battle-hardened staff. At a respectable distance, in every sort of conveyance, followed a jostling, babbling crowd of greedy sutlers and adventurers. To Bonesteel these flapped along like vultures to swoop down upon the North Country so soon to be under British rule again. Apparently their plans were made even before the battle was fought.

"You're all washed up, Teach," the boss bellowed. "And after you've feasted your eyes on Sir George enough, turn yourself around and view the fleet."

They were hauling the fleet. The great *Confiance* was shaking out her sails to catch the wind, if there was any. She was running out what guns she had mounted, and was being moved slowly but steadily up the river. One by one the other ships were hauled into line: the *Finch,* the *Linnet,* and the *Chub.* And there were the dozen armed galleys beating the slow stubborn river with their long oars. As they passed they cut off the sun, and Bonesteel stood in the cold shadow.

Now there were cheers from ships to shore and back again. The confident guns saluted one another. Bonesteel had all he could do to keep from dropping his eyes. He would not be ashamed, although this could be the end of his world, after all.

The boss laughed. "And now that you're all worked out here, I've no doubt that England it will be for you."

The same moon that had come up blood-red behind Mt. Mansfield in Vermont two hours before was now well above Isle aux Noix. A September moon it was, the kind that in another world and another time Bonesteel remembered sailing under.

But now he was almost too weary to remember. He only wondered vaguely why Amos was so fidgety about the moon. He tried to figure out why Amos had said to him at supper, "Teach, you're a-going to get no sleep tonight. This is your last night here. Eat all you can 'cause you're going to work like you've never worked before."

They were getting supplies. A farmer had dumped a load of potatoes by the river where the road from the east came down out of the forest to the water's edge. Bonesteel was rowing the potatoes to the island. He had to pick them up by the handfuls, throw them into the scow, row them, unload them, sack them—and go back for more. It was typical prisoner-of-war labor, inefficient and backbreaking.

The sulky guard who had come along, and Amos, made the boat unnecessarily heavy. The guard wanted to know why the potatoes couldn't wait until morning. "Heh?" He twisted up his face, drew back his lips, exposed his long yellow teeth, and sniffed mightily.

Amos explained that the farmer who brought the potatoes was waiting for his receipt because he had said he didn't trust the British any more than he did the Yankees.

"And where's the lop-eared farmer now?" the guard demanded.

"Back up the pike a piece," said Amos.

"No doubt he's sleeping."

"If them snores means anything, he is."

The guard sniffed. "Devil's foot! Wish I was doing the same. How many potatoes is they?"

Amos giggled. "About a ton."

The guard shifted his musket angrily. "Ton? How many is left?"

"About half a ton."

"Jumping geehemus!" The guard's eyes were large in the moonlight.

Bonesteel, pulling sluggishly at the heavy oars, suddenly came awake. Why had Amos said only half of the potatoes had been transferred? There was only one trip left. If the guard hadn't been so lazy he could have seen that for himself.

When the boat grounded, the guard roused himself. "Guess I'll have me a look at them potatoes, myself."

Amos replied, "Hoped you would. There's something about them I don't just comprehend."

"I'll comprehend 'em for you, you dumb—" The guard clumped over the seats and stepped ashore. "Say! There ain't no half ton there! Say, what's—"

Bonesteel saw a long shadow glide up behind the guard. There was a heavy blow. The guard pitched forward. Matthew Standish was standing over his body, while farther back Jack and Joshua were standing by the farmer's cart.

The sun was coming up in Alburg, Vermont, when the cart stopped at the wharf. Mr. Benson was running toward them. And there, back of him, with her mains'l neatly stopped down, was the *South Wind*, rocking gently at wharfside.

Bonesteel let out a long tired sigh. "What if—? Well, thank God we're back. And thank you all for what you have done."

Matthew got down stiffly. "That sounds like a prayer, Hosea."

"The first of it was, Matthew, for good friends when you need them." Bonesteel looked into Amos's anxious face. "Forgive me, Amos, for not understanding."

Amos's reply was gentle. "No cause you ask that, Mister Teach. You saved my life once. Remember?"

Bonesteel seized Amos's arm in a quick nervous grip. "I said, 'Forgive me, Amos.'"

"Sure now, sure now. What you needs is a good long rest."

Bonesteel dropped his hand. His face was drawn with fatigue. "Sorry," he whispered. "I guess I do."

17

WHILE THE OTHERS talked hour after hour, Bonesteel slept fitfully. At times, as though in a dream, he heard his friends' low voices. At times they soothed him; at times they made him restless. Words like: "He'll have valuable information for the Commodore and the General" . . . "The Carcajou" . . . "Jack's father" affected him one way or the other, or not at all.

At last he woke up and leaned back against the coaming. He watched Jack handle the tiller. He closed his eyes. His head was only clear enough to know that all this was good.

The *South Wind* was now in one of the lake's most beautiful reaches, the Vermont side of lower Lake Champlain. Isle aux Noix, the marching armies, the fleet, the boss, were all far, far away. Bonesteel thought he ought to ask Jack about the Pilot. But he could not yet. It would take a little time.

Jack was speaking to him. "The fusee is in the cabin, Mister Teach. My father brang him back to me in Plattsburg where I stay with Joshua."

"Oh?... Oh yes," Bonesteel replied without enthusiasm.

It would have been foolhardy to enter the main channel while it was still light. That part of the lake was now between the British and American fleets. The shoreline where they landed was on the northern tip of South Hero Island. It was a kind of island-locked lake within the lake. They were about five miles due east from Goose Pond Swamp.

Amos and Matthew built a fire and were going about the business of preparing supper. When everybody had eaten, Matthew brought Bonesteel up to date, and concluded by saying that everything had worked out just the way the General had planned. "You must have really convinced Potts that he was safe. I don't see how you did it in the time you had, and the way you were feeling."

Bonesteel said grimly, "I guess I did. I don't remember about it."

Matthew said that was natural.

Mr. Benson looked up from the fire. "What *I* was going to say was I wish Jack's father was here instead of with the Carcajou. I think he should be here. I think he would be if he could."

Matthew said, "It was him that brought us word about you being taken to Canada, Hosea."

Mr. Benson said, "I reckon we all like Jack's father. I reckon we'd all like to know him better. Hosea, you were right all along."

Bonesteel saw Joshua lean so that his shoulder touched

Jack's. He saw Jack sit up straight and proud. More alert now, Bonesteel listened closely while Matthew stood up and said, "When I think of the wickedness of that Carcajou!"

Bonesteel watched the firelight play on his strong towering figure. "It appears," Matthew said, "that sometimes good folks think thoughts such as in ordinary times would be outside the laws of God and man."

Mr. Benson said, "But these aren't ordinary times, Matthew."

"They are not, friend Benson. What with the British invading us and seizing our property and people; what with honest God-fearing folks trying to build homes in a new land—and this hell-sent thorn in the flesh, Carcajou, preying upon them—"

"And no man's peacetime law strong enough to put him down." The words came out of Bonesteel without his even knowing it.

Matthew's voice was deep and strong. "I don't think we folks here would be wrong in judging him at a time like this."

Bonesteel's eyes were unnaturally bright. "You judged that guard mighty quick!"

"That was immediate necessity. It was his life or ours."

Bonesteel demanded, "So? What's the difference? What about Jack's father? What about me? I say the Carcajou should die!"

Bonesteel knew they were all looking at him. Matthew cautioned, "A man should think carefully before he talks like that. It would lie against his conscience as long as he lives if he didn't speak truly."

Bonesteel was aware that Joshua had leaped up. "I too say the Carcajou should ought to die."

Bonesteel looked hard at Matthew, and he heard Jack say, "Mister Teach knows my knife wait the chance."

Then it was Amos, standing there clenching his fists until they shook. "I been a slave. White folks don't cotton to black folks killing white folks nohow. . . . But the Carcajou he killed my wife; he killed her before my face and eyes." Amos's voice rose higher. "If'n I gets the chance I'll kill him with my two hands. I'm a free man. I'll kill him with my own two hands, so help me God!"

Hard-eyed, Bonesteel glared at Matthew's troubled face, glared as Matthew raised his arms and said, "Let us seek His guidance."

Matthew prayed, "Our God, who art the father of all men who try to do your will, what must we do now?"

Matthew threw out his arms and cried, "Give us a sign, Father! Give us a sign!"

Bonesteel leaped up. "A sign? I'm the sign! For Amos and Jack and the Pilot, I am the sign!"

Matthew recoiled. "Hosea! You are feverish!"

Bonesteel laughed harshly at him.

Matthew pleaded, "Do not tempt God that way, Hosea. Perhaps I went too far. The General has ordered the *Black Sloop* Gang captured, now that they have served his purpose. Perhaps that's the way—"

139

"The General?" Bonesteel shouted, "Then he'll get to the Carcajou before I do."

Matthew replied, "Yes, that's right."

"Then it's tonight! Now! What do you think I've been thinking about all this time?"

"Where is he?" Amos shouted.

Jack said, "In the swamp."

Bonesteel looked at Matthew. "Now what do you say?"

Matthew looked away and waited a long moment. At last he said, "All right. It must be all right."

It was the same fire; the same mussy camp; the same cook and Laroque; and the same Lycurgus Potts blustering at the same menacing Carcajou. Only Hook Nose and Jack's father were not there.

Lycurgus was yelling at the Carcajou, "You got me into this. You and that smooth-talking Hook Nose. Where's my reputation now?"

The Carcajou was looking down contemptuously at Potts's now badly torn and smeared fancy clothes. "Why don't you shut up?"

Lycurgus must have been desperate, because he shook his fat finger under the Carcajou's nose. "You talked me into this—me, a practicing Christian."

The Carcajou slapped Potts's mouth, seized him by his tight coat, and raised him so that his toes dangled above the ground. "Ye slobbering little weasel! Could hardly wait, could ye, to get yourself tangled up with Hook Nose's gold?"

140

Frightened, Potts sank his teeth into the Carcajou's hairy arm. The Carcajou let out a roar of pain, and seized Potts's throat. Potts kicked and struggled. The Carcajou threw him to the ground, knelt upon him, and continued to choke him.

Bonesteel slid his gun forward. All that he had suffered went into the long cold bead he drew on the Carcajou's heart.

"Hold it!" someone whispered. A hand closed over the hammer of his gun.

Bonesteel looked up into the sweating face of Matthew Standish. "There's a British gunboat in the bay. They're sending a boat in. Be here any minute." Standish looked up quickly to see what the Carcajou was doing.

The Carcajou was now dragging Potts into the thicket. Bonesteel heard him thrashing his way through, stopping now and then to get his breath. There was a splash. After a while the Carcajou returned alone.

Bonesteel felt Matthew's fingers bite into his shoulder. "Can't afford a shot now. Sh! Here come some of them from the gunboat."

Hook Nose appeared, and with him were two armed sailors. Hook Nose was nervous and in a hurry. In a low voice he demanded of the Carcajou, "Where's Potts?"

The Carcajou was still breathing hard. "Ain't here. What's your hurry?"

"Our army is moving, so there must be American patrols nearby."

141

"Ye can deal with me."

"Potts was to get some exceedingly important information for me. What's delaying him?"

Bonesteel saw that the Carcajou was stalling Hook Nose while he could think things out. "Potts, did you say?"

"Yes. Potts!"

"Oh. Well, Potts has seen fit to absent himself from this here meeting, I guess. So help me. Ain't it the truth."

"Bad for us. Bad for him. He was going to get his last payment, *if* he delivered. A sizable sum."

Apparently that was what the Carcajou was waiting for. He spoke rapidly. "I'll just give ye that there information myself. I've got it right here in Potts's own handwriting—proper and shipshape, as ye might say." The Carcajou fished a soggy piece of paper from his pocket.

Hook Nose took it gingerly. "This thing is all wet!"

The Carcajou looked at the paper in innocent surprise. "Well now, so it is. It must have got wet somehow."

Impatiently Hook Nose squatted down by the fire and opened the paper. " 'Vermont volunteers coming in spite of governor.' " Hook Nose looked up angrily. "Know that." He read again. " 'Three thousand regulars detached to Niagara.' Know that too. Does Potts think we'll sail the fleet over the dew and fight what's left of their army?"

The Carcajou laughed.

Hook Nose barked, "Did I say something funny?" He ran his finger down the sheet. Suddenly his eyes lit up.

"Here, now. Type and number of guns in Macomb's shore batteries. Location of same. Good. Got to know how close our fleet can come to Macomb's establishments."

At last Hook Nose looked up and gave a short nod.

"Ye can pay me," the Carcajou was quick to say. He held out his hand.

Hook Nose jerked his head toward his two armed sailors. "Pay you? . . . On second thought, I don't have to pay anybody, do I?"

The Carcajou drew himself up. "Potts has gave me the go-ahead to collect for him. And he hopes it will be enough to pay for all the risks he has took. God rest his soul."

Hook Nose shot a quick glance. "Eh? What's that you said?" Then he looked down at the paper. "Oh, very well." He produced two gold sovereigns and tossed them at the Carcajou's feet.

Bonesteel saw the crafty leer on the Carcajou's face as he scooped the coins up.

Hook Nose had something else on his mind. "I want you to talk to that confounded Pilot. We need his knowledge."

"What's he done now?" the Carcajou roared.

"Ran us on a reef yesterday."

Bonesteel heard Jack beside him whisper, "Merci le bon Dieu."

Hook Nose jabbed his finger. "You talk to him." He turned to the guard. "Get that man up here."

When the guard pushed Jack's father forward the Carcajou wasted no time. He hit him full in the face. Then he thrust his stubbled jaw close to the Pilot's and hissed and yelled at him so loud Hook Nose had to quiet him down.

Matthew Standish was beside Bonesteel. The Carcajou hit the Pilot again. Standish's eyes flickered. "Steady now, Hosea. We're well armed, and if we work it right—"

But Jack could stand it no longer. He whispered, "I got to do something." And before Standish could stop him he cautiously raised his head and gave the owl call.

The Pilot stiffened. Laroque moved away from the Carcajou.

Hook Nose looked nervously toward the thicket, took a step toward it. Seeing nothing, he turned back to the fire, snapping his fingers impatiently. "Hurry up," he demanded. "Make this old fool understand."

During all this Bonesteel had not noticed that Amos Lash had been creeping forward. Just when the Carcajou drew back his fist to hit Jack's father again, Bonesteel saw Amos leap up, heard him utter a savage cry, saw him extend his arms, hook his fingers like claws, and rush at the Carcajou's throat.

He saw the Carcajou jerk out his pistol and fire. He saw Amos cough and fall.

Jack leaped up, his knife drawn back. The Carcajou jerked out his other pistol.

Bonesteel saw all the rest: Jack's knife burying itself in the Carcajou's upraised arm, the Carcajou's pistol going off harmlessly in the air. And the Carcajou pulling the knife out and throwing it on the ground.

144

Then everything happened at once. Hook Nose grabbed the Pilot and kicked a bucket of water over the fire. Bonesteel rushed forward to use his musket as a club. There were shots and shouts, and a melee which moved rapidly toward the water's edge. And then Bonesteel found himself and Jack standing helplessly on the shore.

Not far offshore, but far enough, was the *Black Sloop*. A skiff had just put the German cook and Laroque aboard her, and was pulling toward the gunboat.

Then, as the hated enemy craft pulled away, Bonesteel saw the Pilot at the rail. Jack again gave the forlorn cry of the owl.

His father did not reply, but just stood there looking hopelessly toward the shore.

18

THAT NIGHT they sewed Amos's body in the *South Wind's* spare jib. At Matthew's nod they lifted him over the side of the boat and buried him "at sea" in the deep channel off Gravelly Point.

There were stinging tears in Bonesteel's eyes when Matthew tried to comfort him by saying, "Amos will find his wife a-waiting for him on yonder Jordan's shore, Hosea. Perhaps 'tis better that way."

But Bonesteel blamed only himself for Amos's death.

So Matthew tried to talk about something else. "There's Fort Izard, Hosea."

Bonesteel didn't care to answer.

"All that work for nothing. General Macomb's cleaned it out. Moved everything to the forts in town." Bonesteel felt Matthew's gentle hand on his arm. "You didn't answer, Hosea. . . . Here, friend, let me take the tiller. . . . Amos had to go. God's ways are not man's ways."

Bonesteel swayed loosely with the motion of the boat. He mumbled, "And they even got Jack's father."

"We must have great faith now," Matthew said.

"Faith? . . . Did you see Jack's face when we came back from seeing the British taking his father away?"

"I did."

"And did you see Amos drop when the Carcajou shot him?"

Matthew's voice was unruffled. "Yes, I did."

Bonesteel seized Matthew's arm. "And the Carcajou got away!"

"That's right, Hosea."

Bonesteel cried out in agony, "It's all my fault, Matthew. I've made a mess of everything. Set the course, Matthew; I can't go on." He slumped forward.

Matthew's voice drifted to him just as though Matthew were talking to himself. "I'll take us all across channel to Mother's place. A good sleep will come in right handy. . . . I reckon the Commodore can wait for your information. The British won't be coming up the lake on a south wind. Mother will tell us if the wind changes. We've all got to get some sleep. Especially you—Mister Teach."

The next morning Bonesteel told everybody he felt fine, and that he was now in as good condition as he had ever been.

Of course there was a heavy ache in his heart, which he didn't talk about. But when the *South Wind* doubled Cumberland Head that afternoon and he saw spread out before him a vast stage already filled with the tense drama of men and ships, he told himself he too was ready. He was ready and eager to fight the British.

Plattsburg Bay lay before him like a great saucer of

water, about two miles across in any direction. To the north was a long sand beach, and at the center of it, at Dead Creek, Matthew told him, was a small American battery. To the northeast jutted the pine- and cedar-clad Cumberland Head. To the southeast was the open lake. To the southwest lay Crab Island. To the west was the New York mainland and Plattsburg.

His eyes sought the new and unfamiliar. Over Plattsburg hung a heavy pall of smoke out of which issued the slow rumble of cannonade. But the smoke was too dense to be only cannon smoke. Even at that distance there was the smell of burning wood. At least part of the town must be on fire. Reluctantly Bonesteel dragged his eyes away to search for the fleet.

There it was a mile to the west, fantastically tall, appearing to be suspended in the air above the water. That was a trick of the sun on the water. Then he heard Matthew say, "Come on, friends, into it." As he made his approach the fleet settled down on the water where it belonged.

Bonesteel said, "Matthew, what's that new ship at the head of the line?"

"That's the *Eagle*. She wasn't at King's Bay. Just been commissioned."

Jack said, "The others are there, Mister Teach. The *Saratoga,* the *Ticonderoga,* and the *Preble*. They good to see again, yes?"

Bonesteel laughed and even tousled Jack's hair. "Yes —you young Indian." Jack grinned back.

Matthew laughed at that. "While you're feeling so good, don't overlook the gunboats." He pointed to the line of familiar row-galleys, in the half-distance, flying toward the long beach at the north of the bay. "How many do you make, Benson?"

Mr. Benson stood up and ticked them off with his finger. "One—two—three—I make seven. Shouldn't there be ten?"

Bonesteel pointed north to the tree-backed beach. "Look there, off Dead Creek. There's one."

At that instant Bonesteel saw a small cottony ball of cannon smoke bloom up from the lone craft.

"Firing at Dead Creek bridge," Matthew said. "British must have taken our battery there. That means they've broken through."

A puff of smoke answered from the scrub on shore. White water leaped up close to the galley.

Bonesteel got extremely excited. "Good heavens! They'd better claw off. . . . Claw off!" he yelled. "If you get too far inshore—it's shallow in there!" How his heart was pounding. Did Matthew look at him closely while saying, "There now, Hosea, they'll pull out all right. See, they're doing it now?" Bonesteel tried to relax.

It was Jack who found the other two galleys. He pointed to the west. "There are the others."

Those two were heaving shot at a long roll of dust hovering over the shore road leading to town. Forcing himself to be calm, Bonesteel said, "Must be a whole regiment of Redcoats strung out along there. Probably some of the same troops I saw in Canada. . . . Well, enough of this. Let's get to the *Saratoga*."

Once again Bonesteel was on the quarterdeck of the great American flagship *Saratoga*. His friends were standing in a semicircle around him. He was facing Commodore Macdonough.

To himself, Bonesteel thought the Commodore greatly changed. He seemed much graver and more gaunt. The Scotchman's twinkle was gone from his eyes. Instead there was an urgency there, almost a desperation, and an impatient iron quality, like a will to win against impossible odds.

Without the usual preliminary light talk the Commodore said, "My lieutenant tells me you say you have important information for me."

Bonesteel replied, "Yes sir. I have exact information about the entire British fleet."

"That's a large statement, schoolmaster. Everybody else seems to know everything about the British fleet except me, these days." Then Macdonough was looking at the long fresh scar on Bonesteel's head. He was pointing at it. "Is that part of the story?"

Macdonough had made Bonesteel nervous and jumpy again. But, controlling himself, he said, "In a way, it is."

Matthew stepped in to help. "Hosea here has had a rough time, Commodore. But we know he can tell you just what he says he can. He's been a prisoner at Isle aux Noix. They made him work on the fleet, especially the

Confiance. Sort of sat in the front pew, you might say."

The Commodore's manner became less curt. "I see. Then in that case I should be grateful, Mr. Bonesteel. About their army we know quite a lot, thanks to Standish here, and others. But we don't know very much about their fleet. . . . What's the tonnage of their *Confiance?*"

"Twelve hundred, sir."

"Continue, please."

"She carries a crew of three hundred and twenty-five. She can throw a broadside of four hundred and eighty pounds. She's pierced for thirty-nine guns, but all of them weren't mounted when she got away."

The Commodore lifted his eyebrows. "The guns?"

"Twenty-seven long twenty-fours, four thirty-two-pound carronades, and six twenty-four-pound carronades."

The Commodore pursed his lips and let his eyes range his own ship. "The *Confiance* is heavy. I'd say she's in our Constellation class." Then he was asking for the *Confiance's* measurements.

Bonesteel gave the figures rapidly. "Length, one hundred sixty-three feet; beam, forty feet; depth in hold, thirteen." He jerked his head from side to side as he spoke. "They talked a lot," he said stiffly.

Again the Commodore was looking at the scar on Bonesteel's head. "Had your eyes open, didn't you?" Then he said, "I don't like to keep you standing here in the sun like this. But I have to know everything. What impressions did you get?"

Bonesteel straightened up and went on mechanically,

151

"She has oversized fighting tops. There's a furnace for hot shot. They talked a lot about sharpshooters against us, and setting us on fire."

"She'll certainly try; we expect that. But what were your impressions?"

Bonesteel looked down at the deck to steady himself, and then he looked off at the galleys which by now were all engaged. "I wouldn't want you to take my ideas for any more than they're worth."

The Commodore's voice was kind. "I'm asking, Mr. Bonesteel."

Bonesteel licked his lips. "All right. I don't think they'll be ready to fight with all they've got."

"Why do you say that?"

"The captain who took the fleet out of the Richelieu isn't the one who will command her. That will be a Captain Downie. And they say there's a bad feeling between Downie and Prevost. . . . The crews are green and don't know their officers. They haven't had time to work together. But they're all overconfident. I think Downie will make a mistake."

The Commodore looked so long at him that Bonesteel got angry. He thrust his jaw out. "That's my opinion. You asked me."

The Commodore smiled. "As a matter of fact, you've told me just what I've wanted to know. Battles are lost and won because somebody makes a mistake, Mr. Bonesteel. And I am now in a position to help this Downie make his. They'll be tough. And they'll fight. But I'll watch for that mistake. Does that make you feel any better?"

Bonesteel grinned weakly, and nodded. Then he told the Commodore about the other three British ships and the twelve gunboats. After that he knew he should have left. But he still had something he had to say.

"Commodore Macdonough, sir?"

"What is it, Mr. Bonesteel?"

"Would there be a place for me on this ship when the battle comes?"

"You have a score to even up, I take it? But you look ready for sick bay to me, schoolmaster."

"It would mean a lot to me to fight the *Confiance* on this lake from this ship," Bonesteel said stubbornly.

"It's true I'm shorthanded. I've even got some of the General's regulars here. He's also sent me about twenty military prisoners who want to fight. Yes sir, I could use you and anybody else you could find. But I still strongly advise you to go somewhere and go to bed. You've done your part. The General would agree with me there. You see, I know quite a bit about you."

Throughout all this speech Bonesteel saw his friends were looking back and forth from the scar on his head to the Commodore. And he knew the Commodore, polite but skeptical, was not intending to accept what he was going to say next. But he hoped his voice would not rise hysterically, and spoil it.

"I *have* got a score to settle, sir. There's a good man pressed in that British fleet—and there's Hook Nose—

and there's the Carcajou! And it's all wrapped up in that *Confiance!* I've got to fight on this ship! I've got—I've got—"

Bonesteel felt himself falling, and strong arms steadying him.

Dimly he saw the Commodore, and heard him say, "Mr. Bonesteel is a sick man, gentlemen. You just don't get over a head wound that quickly."

19

LYING THERE on his blankets, Bonesteel
looked up through the trees and gave up
trying to figure it all out.

Mr. Benson had brought him a bowl of soup, and had
said, "This has only got beans and a little salt pork. All
I could get, but it's hot."

Bonesteel had drunk what he could and had fallen
back. "Where am I?"

"Crab Island. And you ought to see the place. Hundreds of men lying around all forlorn and ragged and
sick. The General sent 'em over from the forts on the
mainland. Some's got shelters, and some hasn't. Dang
the British!"

"What are they sick with?" Bonesteel had whispered.

"Oh, the usual—flux—and there's a little pox."

"That's the way with an army."

"Yep. And lots of them's just boys and homesick."

"Any doctors?"

"Not near enough."

Cannon had rumbled in the distance. Bonesteel had
tried to rise up again, but he was too tired.

Mr. Benson had rambled on. "Strange, isn't it? Come all the way from home to fight a battle, and then they'll probably spend their time on their backs, sick, on Crab Island, right in the middle of it."

It was dark when Bonesteel woke up again. Low voices came to him from a small fire nearby. He opened his eyes. Matthew, Joshua, and Jack were talking to Mr. Benson.

Matthew was asking, "How's our friend Mister Teach?"

"Been asleep since yesterday. Never saw a man sleep so," Mr. Benson replied.

"It's not unusual." Then Matthew changed the subject. "As I was saying, General Macomb is burning the barracks and the hospital buildings at the forts. Plans to burn one or two buildings every night."

"Now why does he do a fool thing like that?" Mr. Benson wanted to know.

"For the smoke, friend Benson. He has regulars marching in, out of the smoke, and out again through it, so the British will think it's those Niagara troops coming back."

Bonesteel heard Matthew go on about how the General was sending out working parties every night to plant trees in the roads coming up on the forts from the south, and building new roads that led off nowhere, so as to fool the British if they attacked from that direction—which Matthew thought they would.

Bonesteel closed his eyes. He could hardly keep his

interest up. Vaguely, he heard Mr. Benson say something about, "Suppose that Redcoat Prevost beats Macomb anyway?"

Matthew seemed to say it wouldn't make any difference so long as the British didn't get control of the lake. And Mr. Benson said that he saw that all right, and had then said that the key to everything was the American fleet out there in the bay.

Something clicked in Bonesteel's head. He sat bolt upright. "Macdonough and I will lick 'em all," he shouted. Then he fell back exhausted. What good did that do? He, Bonesteel, would be helpless.

When Bonesteel woke up next morning, Mr. Benson came to him with some fried perch. He asked, "Hosea, did you hear anybody around last night?"

Bonesteel said he wouldn't have known and wouldn't have cared if anybody had even stepped on his face.

"Well, I can't understand it," Mr. Benson fretted on. "When I got up there were these fish, three dozen of them, cleaned and boned, and wrapped up as neat as you please."

"Maybe the others know."

"They weren't here all night. Been helping at the forts."

"Well, then, we've got an unknown friend, though little I care . . . unless you think I got up and caught them?" Bonesteel didn't care whether he sounded sarcastic or not.

Mr. Benson sat down beside him, and explained patiently. "I didn't tell you, Hosea, but this note was with the perch."

Bonesteel snatched the note. It was written in a fine hand. It read, "Jack's father was pressed on board the *Confiance*. There is nothing anyone can do."

It must have been very early the next morning, certainly before sunrise, that somebody was throwing an extra blanket over Bonesteel. He was annoyed, and he whispered peevishly, "Go away," thinking it was Mr. Benson.

There was a gentle pressure on his shoulder, and a strange soft laugh penetrating his dreams.

Bonesteel opened his eyes. A sharp sallow face—he knew it was sallow—was bending over him. And there must have been a dangling earring somewhere. Memories of an affair in a swamp, and of a desperate moment on a rolling boat, came to him. . . . And there must be a flashing smile and white teeth.

A voice said softly, "But yes, it's me. The man of principle, your friend, Mister Teach."

"Laroque!" Bonesteel tried to get up as he had tried once long before.

"The same. But do not arise."

Bonesteel sank back. "How long have you been here?"

Laroque must have been rolling his tongue in his cheek and looking impish. "Um—since before Mr. Standish and Jack and Joshua go."

"That was two or three days ago."

"Most certainly."

For some reason, weak as he was, Bonesteel began to laugh. That made Laroque laugh too.

Mr. Benson woke up. "Hosea, are you delirious? . . . Or are you talking to somebody?"

Bonesteel put a teasing note into his reply. "I'm talking to the most dangerous rascal still alive on Lake Champlain."

"What?" Mr. Benson's jaw must have dropped away down.

"Laroque! The man who saved my life."

Laroque was having fun too. He said, "It is true. I did a few favors."

Mr. Benson snapped angrily, "It seems that I am called upon to meet the strangest people."

Laroque clicked his tongue sympathetically. But the way his voice sounded made Bonesteel think there must be an irrepressible twinkle in his eye. "Is that so hard to do, sir?"

" 'Tis a pity Matthew Standish is not here. I dare say he'd not laugh."

Bonesteel laughed all the harder.

Laroque put unexpected kindness in his voice, like the man who forgives quickly because he understands. "Do not feel so bad, Mr. Benson. . . . Can you see that I have here six fine partridges for you and Mister Teach?"

"Humph!" was Mr. Benson's reply.

"The food on this island!" Bonesteel could almost see Laroque shudder. "That you should feed it to a sick man."

"What did you expect?" Mr. Benson barked. Then he softened a little. "Well, thank you for the partridges, anyway."

"You are welcome, sir."

In the dim half-light Bonesteel saw Mr. Benson snatch the gift and turn away. Then he turned back. His voice softened more.

"Why did you come here, Laroque?"

Bonesteel, who was still enjoying all this, was surprised to hear unexpected refinement in Laroque's voice.

"To help a good man get well, sir. . . . Now we get breakfast, do we not? Laroque is a very good cook."

20

IT WAS THE Sunday morning of September 11, 1814, and in the cold gray dawn the watch on board the *Saratoga* said it first: "Northeast wind, northeast wind! This is the day!"

Then on Crab Island the words were repeated until they were rustling among the sick from one end of the island to the other. "Northeast wind's a-blowing. This is the day they'll be coming."

At the forts it was perhaps some lonely sentry drawing his damp coat closer, glancing fearfully at the blood-red eastern horizon, and walking faster.

The words raced to every bivouac in the American encampment; reached in through the gunports of the blockhouses and forts; drifted with the river fog to the militia in the woods; leaped the Saranac to bestir the confident British fresh from victories in Europe; aroused the Canadians dreaming of their rich plowed fields sloping to the St. Lawrence, and of their dark spruce forests, and of their roaring rivers.

Back sped the words to lick at the rugged American fleet now awake and ready in the bay. The circuit was complete.

Someone was shaking Bonesteel. "Wake up, Mister Teach. The northeast wind she blow!" Bonesteel opened his eyes and stared the way a man will when someone wakes him up too quickly. "And this is the day the British fleet will come. This is the day of the big fight."

Already the cold fall air was pungent with wood smoke and smells of cooking. Overhead, against a crimson sky, the treetops were bending to the southwest. In the distance the guns were already pounding. They too seemed to know. There was no doubt Captain Downie would bring his fleet on this wind.

Forgetting his physical weakness, Bonesteel got up. All around him were little groups of invalids wolfing down coarse food, or trying to. Their eyes were unnaturally bright. Yet they didn't have the reason to fight he had. Nor were they tormented the way he was.

Bonesteel was aware that Mr. Benson was hopping around excitely. "We're going to fight, Hosea. We're going to fight," he kept repeating so much that Bonesteel knew he must be a little out of his head.

Laroque was thrusting food at him.

As he ate he listened to the increasing gunfire at the forts pace the rising sun. His head came up. Over there to the south there was a spate of musket fire. The British must be trying the fords of the Saranac. Jack and Joshua and Mr. Standish would be there. And Jack would be using Bonesteel's gun, which he had borrowed.

Bonesteel would have to do something. He could make it to the northern end of the island where the

General had placed the gun the *invalides* were to serve —where Mr. Benson would be when the battle began.

Bonesteel snatched up his telescope, the one Mr. Benson had brought him from the *South Wind* the day before, and started out.

It was a good gun, he could see that, but even his inexperienced eye told him it would not carry to where the British fleet would probably anchor.

The old gunner was fussing around the gun, and jawing to himself. The invalid crew were standing raggedly at their positions waiting for him to finish. Then the gunner gave an order and the practice routine began. Bonesteel remembered that sort of thing on board the *Saratoga* at King's Bay. He looked longingly at the American fleet far out there on the water, and waited as best he could for the crew to finish. Laroque came up quietly beside him.

"Powder—ram wadding—ram ball! Jump aside lively —now my linstock—boom!" the old gunner shouted.

"Do you think you'll get any fighting in here?" Bonesteel asked the gunner when he had finished.

"Eh? Oh, you're that Mister Teach that got took to Canada.... Well, to tell you the truth, Mister Teach, I don't reckon we'll get a chance to shoot at anything solider than wind. If I was a young man, and able, I'd get me out there on that fleet so quick it would make you blink."

Bonesteel pulled out his telescope and focused it on the *Saratoga.*

163

The gunner came up behind him and squinted over his shoulder. "Out there's where the fighting is going to be." The gunner's wheezy old breath pushed on the back of his neck.

Bonesteel nodded his head and tightened his jaw. He was out there again himself, on the quarterdeck telling Macdonough how much he hated the *Confiance* and how much he wanted to be on the *Saratoga* when the fight started.

A British shore battery coughed at the fleet. The shot fell short. Laroque said, "When the British fleet come the Commodore will be between two fires. What does he do now, Mister Teach?"

Bonesteel handed Laroque the telescope and sat down on a rock.

Laroque put the glass to his eye. "He is on the quarterdeck. He is looking up . . . he is praying! Do you wish to look?"

"I can see the picture in my mind."

"They are all standing facing him . . . he is through now."

Bonesteel watched Laroque hand the glass to the gunner and walked away to stand by himself.

The gunner exclaimed, "Two British officers riding hard over there by Dead Creek. Keep pointing back and shouting something. Now what—?"

Bonesteel leaped up and snatched the glass. "It's their fleet!"

"Those officers must have come from the Lake Road north of the Head." He focused the telescope. "Ah yes, I see them now. They're heading for town to tell Prevost the fleet is coming."

"No doubt of it," the gunner said.

"If I were only strong enough"—Bonesteel started to say, when Jack came running up. "Come quick, Mister Teach, Matthew has been shot! Joshua and I brang him here."

Bonesteel hurried as fast as he could after Jack. They arrived in time to find a surgeon dressing a deep flesh wound in Matthew's thigh. What the surgeon was saying didn't mean much to Bonesteel, but seeing Matthew lying there, sweating against the pain he had just been through, did mean a great deal. Bonesteel felt the terrific emotional storm inside himself which made him burst out strong and clear, "Benson, take me out to the *Saratoga* in the *South Wind!*"

Matthew reached up. "Hosea, you're not fit. Better stay here with me."

"Take me out!" Bonesteel shouted.

Matthew's long gaze was on him. "All right. Maybe that's the only thing to do. Your country is bigger than the Pilot, or Amos, or the way you feel about Hook Nose or the Carcajou. And that's the only way you'll get well, too, because at a time like this your country is bigger than anything else. I'm not ashamed to put it that way."

Bonesteel looked down at Matthew's serious face. "Nor am I ashamed to hear it, Matthew, because that's the way it's been in the back of my mind all the time, I guess."

With his usual twisted smile, Laroque asked, "Mister

165

Teach would not object if I accompanied him? I am sure his country would accept my—shall I say—odd talents, without asking too many questions?"

Jack was on his feet. "And me also." He went to the tree against which he had leaned Bonesteel's gun. "Here, Mister Teach, you carry it."

Joshua said, "Count me in, too, Mister Teach."

Bonesteel had been watching Matthew listening to all this, which had been said in the light way men will talk when they are speaking of great personal danger and great personal sacrifice for a great cause.

But he was not surprised when Matthew said, "I would have liked to go with such a company of brave hearts. But at least I can pray for you, which I shall do most heartily."

Bonesteel smiled and said, "That's all right, Matthew. But don't pray for the *Confiance*."

21

BONESTEEL WAS spokesman. "We have come to help, if there's a place for us on board, sir."

He was aware of the Commodore's penetrating glance. "There's a place." The Commodore gave an order. "Take these men to the captain of marines. He will issue them muskets. . . . Ah, I see you have a fine weapon there, Mr. Bonesteel." He changed the order. "Three muskets. And then put Mr. Bonesteel and his friends in the main top. They can give valuable service as sharp-shooters."

It didn't take long. Soon Bonesteel found himself and his friends, with several others, in the spacious mainmast fighting top. Looking down, he could range the decks of practically all the American ships. If he chose to look out and to the west he could see the General's forts, or to the east his eye could come pretty close to topping the pines on Cumberland Head. To the south he did see, about a mile away, the *South Wind* winging back to Crab Island.

But it was to the lookout far above him that his eyes

returned, for it was from the lookout that would come the first word of the British fleet.

Suddenly this man threw himself forward, shielded his eyes, and peered intently eastward.

"He sees them," Bonesteel exclaimed.

The lookout cupped his hands and bawled down to the quarterdeck far below, "Sail ho! Sail ho!"

It was the Commodore who called back, "Where away?"

The lookout jabbed his arm toward Cumberland Head. "Yonder off the starboard beam beyond the Head, sir."

Macdonough exaggerated a great nod.

Now the lookouts on the other ships were singing out, and Bonesteel knew they had spied what must have been the tips of the enemy masts moving along steadily beyond the distant pines.

Throughout the fleet everybody was looking toward the Commodore. He was raising his megaphone to his mouth. The only sound Bonesteel could hear was the wind sighing through the rigging. The Commodore shouted, "They will be here soon! . . . We are ready! . . . Every man will do his best."

No shouting response as there had been at King's Bay. Even the wind seemed to drop. But Bonesteel understood. Every man down there was doing the same thing he was doing—looking quickly around at his neighbor, and then looking long inside himself, and testing himself against the odds, and finally saying to himself, "This is worth fighting for."

In another half hour the British fleet was swinging

away down around Cumberland Head Reef, working back, and anchoring just out of reach of the American carronades.

But Bonesteel watched only the *Confiance*.

A halfhearted retching from the enemy's guns came to him.

Some of the landsmen below laughed. Nobody had told them. Distantly Bonesteel heard the Commodore call out, "Scaling their guns! ... Reduced powder charges! ... First time they've been fired. ... Won't be so gentle next time!"

Somewhere there was a nervous laugh again, and this time someone said gently, "Easy, matey. Just take it easy —just take it easy."

A captain's gig put out from the *Confiance* and rowed deliberately toward the American fleet. Again the Commodore raised his megaphone, and 820 Americans waited to hear what this piece of bravado might mean.

Macdonough explained, "Captain Downie is looking us over."

Two officers were standing up in the stern. One started swinging his arm and pointing. The other did the same thing. This familiar gesture made Bonesteel's stomach muscles tighten in anger. The Commodore shouted, "The first man is Captain Downie."

The gig crawled back across the sparkling water, and for a moment the unreality of this fantastic business seized upon Bonesteel's mind. How could all this possibly be the prelude to the bloodletting that must surely follow?

Now the enemy ships seemed to talk among themselves. And now they seemed to reach a decision, for they gathered way again and came on. At first they kept good order, but as they tacked inside the Head a baffling wind threw them into some confusion, a fact which gave Bonesteel great satisfaction.

Bonesteel whispered in Laroque's ear. "The Commodore chooses his position very well. Let's load up. Good for the courage, eh, my friend?"

Why he should whisper, Bonesteel didn't know. But it seemed appropriate.

Then Joshua shouted, "Look! those first two ships sure are making poor work of it to windward. They must have shallow drafts."

Bonesteel nodded. "They do. They're the *Chub* and the *Linnet.*"

Jack spoke for the first time. "I look for my father when the *Confiance* come."

Bonesteel, thinking only of the coming battle, had forgotten all about the Pilot. He gave Jack an understanding look.

The first American gun spoke to get the range. The shot fell short. The *Chub* was either too busy or too wise to reply.

But now the *Linnet* was passing the *Saratoga* so close he could look down on her decks, as in a play, and see her gun crews standing like actors to their positions. He heard a cold order barked. Those men down there snapped alive. The *Linnet* belched a broadside at the *Saratoga*. A shell struck a chicken coop on the *Saratoga's* deck which held a gamecock. The bird squawked and flew to a gun slide, where it crowed defiantly. The Americans took this as a good omen. Their tension of waiting broke. They yelled with the bird. Bonesteel yelled too.

Through all this the *Saratoga* held her fire.

The *Chub* and the *Linnet* anchored opposite the American brig *Eagle*. Bonesteel aimed his gun.

Now came the *Confiance*, frowning, silent, withholding fire. Trial shots from the *Eagle* and the *Saratoga* struck the water near her. Bonesteel looked down. He saw the Commodore, himself, aim and fire a twenty-four-pounder. He jerked his head up, trying to follow the ball. Men and equipment flew asunder as the shot ranged the hated ship's deck. Another shot lifted her port bow anchors and splashed them into the lake. Bonesteel leaped up and shouted, "Come on and fight!" But the *Confiance* continued to come in without speaking a gun.

Near Bonesteel a sharpshooter growled, "Dignified devil, ain't he? ... About three hundred yards, I'd say."

Downie let go his remaining bow and stern anchors.

It was Laroque who shouted, "Hang on!"

A sheet of flame leaped from the *Confiance's* entire broadside battery of double-shotted twenty-fours. Timbers cracked on the *Saratoga*, and deadly splinters whirred through the air. The tornado-like impact slapped the *Saratoga* over so far she rolled her port rail under the water. While he still held on Bonesteel got a quick picture of men falling to the deck far below and sliding helplessly into the scuppers. He heard their cries. It came to him that in that first awful moment many of his countrymen down there were dying. Then fierce healthy anger broke loose in him and he was on his feet yelling defiance with all the rest, and firing and loading and firing at the *Confiance*. The battle, his battle, had begun.

Someone beside him shouted, "Tarred hats, Mister Teach, and striped jerseys, that's what to shoot at."

Someone else shouted, "Uh-huh. There black spot," and squeezed a trigger.

After a while Bonesteel shouted back, "Hot, isn't it?" He worked his tongue around his dry lips and got the taste of burnt powder. "I'm thirsty."

"It's the guns that make it so hot." That was Joshua.

The sharpshooter elbowed him and pointed to a bucket. "There's water there." Bonesteel gulped down a drink, and felt new strength. He became aware of something else. He set down the bucket. "Listen," he cautioned. He turned his head this way and that to get the direction. "Firing slacking off somewhere. . . . To the north."

Everybody looked around with that animal-like alertness men develop in battle, their eyes making ghastly islands in their powder-blackened faces. Through the smoke Bonesteel saw an enemy ship drifting on a course which would bring her down between the two fleets. Battered and crippled she was, slashed sails and rigging fluttered uselessly, severed anchor cables trailing in the water, and her ensign coming down.

172

Bonesteel shouted, "It's the *Chub!* She's striking her colors. She's out of it. Look! Her galleys are running for it." He breathed hot and fast when a few American galleys started in pursuit. He pounded the rail angrily when they had to stop and bail for life instead.

Joshua shouted, "The *Eagle* is drifting too. She's bigger than the *Chub!*"

Laroque said it for them all. "So, we are worse off."

Down past the *Saratoga's* lee the *Eagle* came. The sinking galleys had to lurch and claw to get out of her way. It was a disheartening sight. When the mauled ship was abreast the *Saratoga* Bonesteel thought her decks looked as though a clumsy giant had trod them, crushing men and overturning guns.

But there was angry activity aboard the *Eagle.* Her captain was bawling orders, pounding his fists against the rail, and turning now and again to shout across the water to the *Saratoga's* quarterdeck.

Bonesteel leaned close to Laroque's ear. "She's still full of fight, though."

"But yes, Mister Teach. Maybe she pull back in the line somehow below us. We watch?"

This the *Eagle* tried to do. But her position was too far back. Bonesteel looked at Laroque. Laroque shook his head. "That's not good. The *Eagle* she was first placed to protect the *Saratoga* so several ships cannot fire on her at once. Now we get it. The enemy try to board us now, I think."

Soon red-hot shot were crashing into the *Saratoga,* and

while some of her crew were diverted to put out the fires the *Linnet* and the *Confiance* slugged her with a new wave of ball, grape, and musket shot.

Laroque was right. Up from the decks came the cry, "Prepare to repel boarders!"

Bonesteel yelled with the others when marines rushed to the bulwarks. Loading furiously or swinging outward long steel-tipped pikes, or drawing sabers, they waited for the hated boarding boats. He saw them lean against the special storm of lead so viciously launched against them to drive them back.

Nor were the topmen neglected. The enemy knew that they, above all, could make the assault fail. Bonesteel hunkered down and methodically returned the fire.

But out of the corner of his eye he saw that here and there British marksmanship was beginning to tell. One man stood up straight, glassy-eyed, then pitched to the lake far below at just the precise moment when the *Saratoga* rolled so that he missed the deck. Another topman crumpled and hung, somehow, seeming to prefer to watch the battle head down through sightless eyes. . . . And bloody bandages began to appear.

All this Bonesteel saw without feeling. His only reason for living was to kill anything that moved aboard the *Confiance*.

An officer clambered up from the deck. "When they try to board us, shoot them out of their boats. Watch sharp now. It won't be long." A bit of his hat brim flew away. He snatched the hat off. "Confound it! Now I've got to buy me a new hat!" He jerked away the hanging fragment, jammed the hat askew back upon his head. "They'll try to pick you men off first. Don't let them do it." He scrambled back down the ratlines.

Bonesteel laughed. "How are you going to stop them? That would be a miracle." But then, it was a miracle the impossible order got to them at all.

Through the black smoke now arising from the burning *Saratoga* Bonesteel searched the lurid center between the ships for the great frantic bugs, the boarding boats, coming closer and closer. He shouted, "There they are!"

The yelling and howling that came up from below told him what the smoke now prevented him from seeing, that the assault was being desperately pressed and fought off. He could only load and fire until his gun barrel was burning hot in his hand.

At last a bug, two bugs, three—must be creeping away. The yelling told that. The assault must have failed. But he knew others would come.

It was after the repulse of the third assault that Jack shouted, "Something wrong, Mister Teach; we don't fire so much down there."

Fearfully Bonesteel stared down upon the deck, which he could now get glimpses of. It was littered with the debris of dismounted guns and the many dead and dying.

It was true. The *Saratoga* was hardly firing at all. The reason was obvious. And as though to prove her greater strength a heavy shot from the *Confiance* at that moment lifted a cannon lazily into the air and dropped it down the *Saratoga's* main hatch.

But there was some apparent design in the movements of the living. At the bow men were working frantically at the spring line, and at the stern others were moving around the stern capstan, stepping up and down and around through the wreckage.

Then Bonesteel knew. "This is it!" he yelled. "This is where Macdonough takes advantage of the British mistake. Watch! Oh dear God, watch!" He leaped up and shook his musket at the enemy. "You lobsters didn't figure this one, did you? Macdonough's winding ship! Do you hear? He's winding ship!"

Laroque pulled him down to his knees.

The sharpshooter warned in crazy staccato, "Ah-ah— get ready, lads. When we gets our stern around toward those devils they'll throw everything they've got into us. Rake us. Won't be pretty."

Bonesteel still felt Laroque's strong restraining grip. "You keep down, Mister Teach. And keep turning so you can see them. It is quite necessary that we shoot their gun crews. G-e-t r-e-a-d-y." Laroque turned slowly on his knees to show how, took careful aim, and fired.

When the enemy's raking fire struck the awkwardly poised *Saratoga,* stern toward the enemy as she was, Bonesteel knew it was the worst she had got yet. The beset ship groaned and leaped and shuddered and wallowed. It was like throwing shot into a rubble heap. What had already been smashed was smashed more. The men, working down there in that deadly hail, screamed and died. Why the ship herself did not die then and there, hanging uncertainly in that defenseless position, Bonesteel did not know.

But then he began to gasp with relief. It was Jack who was pounding him on the back and shouting, "We made it, Mister Teach! Now we got a new broadside!"

The sharpshooter laughed, "Back to work, boys. We've got 'em now. They can't match that. Macdonough had his anchors all set."

Suddenly Laroque pointed excitedly. "Look there, my friends! Downie is going to try it too."

Bonesteel saw a boat out from the *Confiance*. "Look —look—look! They've got an anchor! If they get that out they'll wind ship just like we did!"

The sharpshooter shouted, "Come on, boys, we'll just pick off that boat crew. The man in front is mine."

It was then that Laroque leaped up in front of them all. With his back fully exposed to the enemy he spread out his arms and screamed, "One moment, sharpshooter! Don't shoot him!"

The sharpshooter shouted, "Get out of the way!"

"No! No!"

The sharpshooter lowered his gun just as Laroque lurched and slid to a sitting position, smiling painfully at Bonesteel.

The sharpshooter aimed again. Laroque whispered, "For the love of le bon Dieu, stop him, Mister Teach."

But Laroque's plea was not necessary, for the man the sharpshooter was about to kill was now standing so all

177

could see, legs apart, and was swinging an axe down upon the hawser bent to the anchor.

"Well, I'll be—" Bonesteel's jaw dropped open.

With one clean cut the man out there severed the hawser.

Bonesteel fell back in disbelief. "He did it!"

Now this crazy unknown hero across the water shook his axe at the *Confiance* and threw it up upon the quarterdeck. Bonesteel saw the shock waves from the *Confiance's* guns lick out and jerk at his hair and shirt; the angry boat crew reaching up at him; heard the mad shouting; the air filled with violence! Splinters were flying from the boat. An oar was leaping from a man's hands. Another was snapping in two. The boat crew was crouching for safety as their countrymen on the *Confiance* fired heedlessly into them, trying to kill the madman who had done this monstrous thing. But in the tumult of it all that man stood there laughing contemptuously. He seemed to Bonesteel to be deliberately tasting the wild flavor of courage in the face of death.

But Bonesteel saw he was not done yet, for now he set the boat to rocking! With that heavy anchor across her bows she was already precariously balanced. Heaving his weight down on one gunwale, he crowded that side under the water. The anchor slipped. He helped it. The boat capsized. He dove free, a clean sweet dive.

Bonesteel threw himself forward. In that last moment of triumph when one man destroyed the British bid for victory, he knew what Laroque had been trying to say.

Jack cried out, "That is my father! That is my father!"

Nodding at Jack, Bonesteel was unaware, for the moment, that Laroque was tugging at his coat. Then he felt it and looked down. Shocked, he dropped to his knees. "You were hit. Oh, Laroque, I didn't know."

"In the back. It doesn't matter. . . . Is the Pilot yet alive?"

Gently Bonesteel drew Laroque close. "Yes, thanks to you. He is alive."

Laroque's voice was weaker. "You remember in the swamp? He say he must do something first?"

"Yes, I remember."

"Now you understand. And Jack understand."

There was a violent movement from Jack. Bonesteel looked up. Jack was leaping for the ratlines. Laroque whispered hoarsely, "Don't let him go."

Bonesteel caught Jack just as he was descending. "Easy, Jack; you can do nothing that way." Jack struggled wildly. "Listen, Jack. You can't save him now. Stay here and fight."

And Bonesteel held him until he said, "I'm all right now."

Jack took up his gun and started firing coldly and methodically. Bonesteel went back to Laroque. But Laroque was dead.

Bonesteel returned to Jack and together they fired on the *Confiance* until her battle flag came down in surrender, and the cease-fire order was given. . . . And Jack would have continued firing if Bonesteel hadn't taken his gun.

22

AFTER THE BATTLE there was much traffic from shore to fleets and back again. People were coming out to see if loved ones were still alive, or to help with the wounded and the dead. Many stayed to man pumps and help plug shot holes to keep the ships from sinking.

Among them was Mr. Benson in the *South Wind*.

Bonesteel, Jack, and Joshua asked permission from the Commodore to leave the *Saratoga*. When Bonesteel told the Commodore they wanted to search for the heroic Pilot, that he was Jack's father, the Commodore urged them to go.

They searched. But by sunset they had to give up. The Pilot must have drowned.

So now they were all together again on Crab Island. It was raining. Mr. Benson had built a fire.

They all tried to comfort Jack. But who could penetrate that grief mask of the ancient Indian people? Jack only wanted Bonesteel to sit quietly with him away from the rest—to share his grief in that way. The others continued to talk in low voices by the fire.

But they hadn't forgotten Jack. They talked about the Pilot's great deed, and what a great man he now was, and how any boy would be proud to have him for a father—thinking that somehow that might ease Jack's grief. But Jack sat silent and straight, seeming not to hear.

Then Bonesteel heard them turn to other things, as men will, even in the presence of grief. They talked about how a battle is said to be a rain maker, and that the rain would probably make it impossible for the General to pursue Prevost if he was retreating, which Matthew thought likely. And then Mr. Benson told how the gun he had served did take a British vessel, the *Chub,* which had drifted out of line.

Bonesteel knew it wasn't because his friends were callous to Jack's grief, but because they had been through a harrowing experience too, and had to talk it out of their systems. It was only natural.

But Bonsteel wasn't really paying much attention. His brain was grappling with something else. He was understanding yet again that in some ways he was not like other men. He felt things more. And he preferred to feel. He could never be satisfied with only the practical aspects of things. . . . And now he was feeling a battle. He was feeling a ship against a ship. He was feeling with a grieving boy who still thought like an Indian, but whose heart could break like a white man's. He was feeling with a "man of principle" who had joined the right side at last and had died like a hero. And he was feeling what the Pilot must have felt in that one glorious moment, erasing all his past weaknesses and acting the man. . . . And Bonesteel was feeling a lake and a valley and a country saved, and a way of life saved. And he was proud, very, very proud, to have been a part of it, even when he was sorrowing with Jack.

Suddenly he heard the talk around the fire become excited. And he heard Mr. Benson slap his forehead and exclaim, "But I saw him through the telescope. May the devil smudge me. I didn't figure it out until now. . . . Jack, Jack! I *don't* think your father *is* dead! I saw Hook Nose make him get into a small skiff and make him row toward Valcour Island!" Mr. Benson came running over to where Jack was sitting, and started shaking him to make him listen. "I even saw Hook Nose launch the skiff from the *Confiance*. He must have been crazy mad to do that. But he did find your father, and he did make him get in. . . . He had a pistol, boy."

They were all standing around Bonesteel and Jack. A series of most un-Indian-like expressions were passing over poor Jack's face.

Bonesteel said, "Are you sure about this, Mr. Benson? It would be an awful thing if—"

Mr. Benson went on where he had left off. "He made him! And then that Hook Nose kept looking back at the *Confiance* until he saw her strike her colors. Then he watched the British gunboats running for it around Cumberland Head as though he wanted to follow but didn't think he could catch up. Then he ordered Jack's

182

father to row toward Valcour. . . . I saw it all through the telescope. But I was so excited about the battle that it all went out of my head as quick as it got in. And I didn't think of it again until now."

The wet dawn was just breaking as they crept to the edge of the woods that came almost down to the water's edge at Smuggler Bay. Even Matthew Standish was there, leaning on a crutch he had made during the battle. He too was armed, because he had said he wouldn't have missed this if it was the last thing he ever did.

The *Black Sloop* was there in the bay. And there was the shack standing shabby and askew on the only open space on shore. A fire was burning in front of the shack. Apparently somebody had been staying awake, or the fire would have been put out by the rain. And the fire made it likely that Hook Nose and the Carcajou, and possibly the cook, were in the shack, instead of on the *Black Sloop*. And they must have the Pilot in there too, Bonesteel thought.

So now all Bonesteel and his friends had to do was keep well hidden, and surround the shack. But what then, Bonesteel wondered? How could they get the Pilot without also risking his life?

Nobody had reckoned on Jack's owl call. Nor was it part of any plan that Jack show himself. But Jack did give the owl call, and he did then step out boldly into the firelight.

183

After a moment of silence the Carcajou came out of the shack, carrying his pistols.

Jack, hand hanging down near his knife, said, "Hello, Carcajou."

Bonesteel saw the Carcajou steady himself as though he didn't believe it, and then say, "Jackie, boy. I knew it would be you to come back."

"Yes, it's me."

"Step closer so's your old friend can see you better."

But Jack stood motionless. "Me, I am here. But I do not see you very well."

The Carcajou licked his lips. "Now if it was that Bonesteel, or any of them other skunks, I'd be afraid of being tricked. But not you, good boy Jack."

Bonesteel saw the Carcajou quietly cock his pistols and step back into the shadow of the door. Bonesteel would have fired but he was afraid of hitting Jack, or perhaps even the Pilot, who might be in the shack.

Jack stepped nearer. "You have the pistols, Carcajou. I come back. But I see you don't trust me."

The Carcajou forced a laugh. "Oh sure. I forgot I had 'em." He relaxed his arms a little.

"You do not put them down. Me, I come back to my fine lonely friend because I hate Mister Teach and Joshua. I like them once, I know better now. But what do I find? My fine lonely friend speak with forked tongue."

"Who, me?"

"Yes, you."

Bonesteel saw the Carcajou's eyes flicker. "Well, now,

184

I can fix that." Carefully he laid the pistols on the ground. "There. See? Now come over here, fine boy Jack."

"Where's the cook?"

"Oh, didn't I tell you about him? He's a quitter. He ran off after the battle."

"Where's Hook Nose?"

The Carcajou made a great act of spitting on the ground. "Him! I'll have no more of him! Them British is all cheaters, losing the battle the way they did. Now they can never pay me no more."

Bonesteel saw the glint of the firelight on metal inside the shack, as though somebody was shifting a musket to a better position.

Jack said lightly, "Have you seen my father, Carcajou?"

"Your fine father, Jackie? No. I do not know where he is."

Jack took a step nearer. "I think he is in the shack."

"You hurt your old friend, Jackie. But you come and see I am not lying. Did I ever lie to you, Jackie?"

"Yes, you have."

Jack took another step. The Carcajou kept a fixed smile as Bonesteel saw him ease himself forward on the balls of his feet, drop suddenly, seize his pistols, and fire at Jack. But Jack was a little quicker. He plunged to the ground and rolled sidewise. The Carcajou leaped up, kicked at Jack, and started running as best he could around the shore to the southernmost point that enclosed the bay.

Bonesteel shouted, "Cover the shack," and started in

pursuit. Then Jack, fleet of foot, passed him. Up ahead, Bonesteel saw the Carcajou fumble frantically with his pistols as he ran.

It was a crazy race around the edge of the bay: the Carcajou, limping rapidly, dodging in and out of the trees, screaming at Jack, and trying to reload one of his pistols; Jack leaping from stone to stone and avoiding the trees to make up time and close the gap, and trying to get into a position to throw his knife; and Bonesteel, seeing it all, and trying to get where he could take aim without hitting Jack.

Now the Carcajou was scrambling up the path which led to the bare promontory at the tip of the point. He burst out into the open. And so did Jack. The Carcajou scrambled to the highest point. Back of him, and straight down, was the lake. Here the Carcajou turned and faced Jack.

"If ye come a step closer, Jack, I'll shoot ye," he screamed.

"The pistols are not loaded, Carcajou," Jack replied.

The Carcajou tipped back his evil red head and laughed. "That is what ye do not know, Jack boy. Now do ye?"

Bonesteel knelt and drew a bead on the Carcajou.

Jack drew back his arm to throw his knife. "Carcajou, for my father you are a dead man." He threw his knife.

Bonesteel fired.

The Carcajou's head jerked back. He clutched at his throat where Jack's knife buried itself. One of his pistols went off harmlessly in the air. He fell backward into the lake.

Bonesteel rushed back to the shack. Heedless of Matthew's warning he ran through the door. Hook Nose raised his gun. Bonesteel knocked it up. The others rushed in.

Bonesteel found the Pilot bound and gagged in the corner.

It was the way Bonesteel wanted it. Before him stood Hook Nose, insane hate on his face, no doubt murder in his heart. Ringed around them were Jack and Joshua, Matthew and Mr. Benson, and the Pilot.

"We *do* meet again, don't we?" Bonesteel said. "But I've got a lot more reason for wanting to finish that fight than I had then." Bonesteel leaped and struck out.

Fists flew only for a moment before the two bitter enemies were rolling on the ground. Each was fighting with released emotions which had been pent up so long. And each was tearing at the other like a savage animal.

Then it was all over. Hook Nose, clothes almost completely torn from his body, was flat on his back, limp and licked. Bonesteel was pinning him down.

Matthew said it for all. "A most gratifying sight."

Bonesteel turned to the others, and panted, "There's only one thing left to do, now."

Bonesteel himself dragged the Carcajou's body from the water, and looked long at the neat bullet hole right between the eyes. "That's what I wanted to know," he said at last. "Now I don't mind going back to being Mister Teach."

About the Author

FRANK A. COOPER was born in Minneapolis, Minnesota. He went to Colgate University, left for two years to take a teaching job in an American missionary school in Austin, Texas, then returned for his degree. Later he received his M.A. in history from Rochester University and has been teaching ever since. He has been writing for many years and has had several plays published.

Mr. Cooper lives on the shoreline of Lake Champlain in a house that he and his wife built mostly with their own hands. He says he "fell in love" with Lake Cham plain the first time he saw it. He has boated along its shores, sailed it, inboarded and outboarded it. He feels that knowing this part of the country so well has made it possible for him to write a living story out of the past, which is what he has done in *Mr. Teach Goes to War.*